THE DRY GULCHER

Wayne D Overholser

CHIVERS

British Library Cataloguing in Publication Data available

This Large Print edition published by AudioGo Ltd, Bath, 2011.
Published by arrangement with Golden West Literary Agency

U.K. Hardcover ISBN 978 1 445 83676 8
U.K. Softcover   ISBN 978 1 445 83677 5

Printed and bound in Great Britain by
MPG Books Group Limited

CHAPTER ONE

Dan Matson was late leaving his ranch for the meeting in Bald Rock, and he would have ridden past the Bailey place without stopping if Mrs. Bailey had not run out of the house, calling, 'Dan! I've got to see you, Dan.'

Irritated, he reined toward her, wondering what Bess Bailey had done now, but when he saw Laura Bailey's face, he realized that something was really wrong, something much worse than one of her daughter's escapades. Terror was in the woman's face, a kind of terror he had never seen there before.

Laura was tough. She had to be to have endured thirty years of hard living in Smith's Hole. She was not an old woman in years, but she was old in experience and her lined face showed it. First there had been the constant danger of Indian attacks, then the outlaw years, and now Justin Albright's threats to make Smith's Hole a winter range for his Skull herd.

He stepped down, asking, 'What happened, Laura?'

For a moment she didn't say anything. She just stood looking at him, the corners of her mouth quivering, then suddenly she whirled toward the log barn, saying, 'There's something in here I want you to see.'

1

He fell into step beside her. He asked, 'Queen Bess in town?'

'I wish you'd quit calling her Queen Bess,' Mrs. Bailey said sharply. 'It makes her furious. If you keep it up, she'll do something she shouldn't.'

'She's done things before she shouldn't,' he said. 'I guess it wouldn't be anything new if she did more of the same.'

He'd grown up with Bess Bailey. They'd ridden together to the Bald Rock school when they were children. After they were grown, he'd taken her to dances and parties. At one time he had been in love with her. Maybe he still was. He didn't know. All he knew for sure was that she wasn't in love with him.

When her father had died three years ago, Bess had decided she was the man of the Bailey family and she was doing her damnedest to prove it. One thing he didn't need, he told himself grimly, was a wife who thought she was a man.

When they reached the barn, Mrs. Bailey opened the door and motioned for Dan to go in. She said, 'Bess has kept old Tip tied up at night ever since the last time he tangled with a porcupine. She says she's pulled the last quill out of his nose that she's going to.

'Well, last night he started barking about one o'clock. I never heard him take on so. Bess lit a lantern and took the Winchester and went out and looked around, but she didn't see anything. After it was daylight she looked some more. She found tracks in the dust here by the door.

'She said it looked to her like a man had ridden up to the barn, then got down and went inside, but she didn't find anything wrong. She came in and told me, so I went with her and we went over every inch of the inside of the barn. Finally we found that hide shoved under the manger of the first stall. It was pushed clear to the back so I wouldn't have seen it if I hadn't got down on my hands and knees.'

He could see the hide now that Mrs. Bailey had pointed it out, but he probably wouldn't have seen it in the gloom of the barn if she hadn't. He pulled it out and unrolled it. It was, as he had expected, a Skull hide.

Mrs. Bailey gripped his arm. 'What do you make of it, Dan?'

'I'm guessing that sometime today Sheriff Douglas will ride in and start looking around,' Dan said thoughtfully. 'Sooner or later he'll find it if you leave it here, and he'll arrest you and Bess for rustling and butchering a Skull steer.'

She nodded. 'That's what Bess said. But why us? Why not you? Or one of the other men?'

'Maybe they figured it was safer to plant it here than on a man. Or maybe they figure to shoot one of us and they didn't want to shoot a woman. Or maybe it's just a warning to go

3

along with the threats Albright has been making.'

She walked through the barn door and stood with her back to the wall, her worried gaze on the cottonwoods that lined Green river half a mile away. When he joined her, she said dully, 'It won't work. It'll take more 'n Albright's threats to push me off the Box B. I've lived here most of my life. I helped Al build this ranch. I gave birth to Bess in the front bedroom of the house and I thought I was going to die. Al did die in that room and he's buried up yonder on the bench. Justin Albright can shoot me if he wants to, but we ain't moving.'

'That might be another reason he started with you,' Dan said. 'Al Bailey was the first settler in the Hole. You were the first woman to come here. You stand for something, Laura, you and Bess. If you left, I'm guessing that most of the other women would make their men go.'

'And that would give old Justin an easy victory.' She shook her head. 'No, we ain't leaving.'

Dan glanced at the rim to the east. 'You know, I've been expecting some dry gulcher to take a shot at me from up there, but it hasn't happened yet. Maybe it's too far to hit a man, but it'd be a damned good warning to go along with this. It just ain't like Justin Albright to keep on talking and not put some teeth into

4

THE DRY GULCHER

his words.'

'What'll we do with the hide?' she asked.

'Leave it where it is,' he answered. 'I'll see the sheriff as soon as he comes down Maroon creek. I might even ride out to meet him. I'll take the wind out of Albright's sails.'

'Suppose he doesn't believe you?'

'He will,' Dan said. 'Albright has Judge Verling in his hip pocket, but he don't have Buck Douglas there. Somebody has tipped him off so he'll know what he's looking for. I aim to find out who did the tipping.'

She sighed. 'I hope so. I wouldn't like it in jail. Neither would Bess.'

'I've seen you come through some pretty tight squeaks, Laura, but I never seen you take anything as hard as this. Why?'

'I've always intended to die in this house,' she said. 'I've got a hunch I ain't going to live much longer. After we found that hide, I told Bess that if they haul me off to the Craig jail, I'll die there. I just can't stand thinking about being locked up in a stinking cell.'

He patted her shoulder. 'You ain't going to jail. After I see the sheriff, I'll ride over to the Little Snake and talk to Lee Jackson. The last I heard, the Skull cattle are grazing just on the other side.'

'And they're headed this way,' she said bitterly. 'It won't do you no good, Dan. Jackson's just the Skull ramrod. He don't give the orders.'

'No, and he ain't as smart as Albright or as mean,' Dan admitted, 'but he'll probably know what the old bat's up to. If he does, I'll get it out of him.'

She shook her head. 'Don't go. Wait until he comes courting Margo Lane again. It'll save you a long ride. Besides, Skull don't like Hole riders. You'll just get into trouble.'

'There won't be no trouble unless I start it,' he said, 'and Jackson ain't coming back to see Margo. Not after what I told him the last time he was here. Well, I'll mosey along. You quit worrying, Laura. You hear?'

'I'll try,' she said.

She wouldn't stop worrying no matter how hard she tried, he told himself as he stepped into the saddle. He was ashamed as he rode away. Words were cheap. It would take more than talk to make her quit worrying.

A mile below the Box B the road swung toward the river. He followed it into Bald Rock, his gaze turning repeatedly to the break in the east rim that marked Maroon creek, the only practical entrance into the Hole. Buck Douglas would come that way, and Dan decided he'd better make his stop at Charley Klein's store a brief one and tell the others what had happened. Bess had probably told them already, but he'd repeat it and let them know what he planned to do.

Bess would faunch around like a wild filly, he told himself grimly. She'd want to bar the

6

Maroon creek gap and station some men to seal off the Hole from the outside world. Some of the others like Lige Carter and Nate Willets would back her up, but it wouldn't work.

No man or group of men can seal themselves off from the rest of the world, and they ought to have sense enough to know it, but Bess would buck anything he proposed just on general principles. It was her way of proving she was a better man than he was and he'd had enough of it.

Dan had known there would be a showdown between the local ranchers and Skull since early summer, when Justin Albright had sent word that he expected to winter his steer herd in Smith's Hole. There had been no agreement as to what form the resistance would take. That was the reason for the meeting in Bald Rock today. Dan guessed that planting the Skull hide under the Box B manger was nothing more than another threat from Justin Albright, and he didn't think Buck Douglas would take it seriously.

Still, he was not as sure as he had tried to make Laura Bailey think he was, and it made him furious that she was upset about it. Albright had offered to buy all of the ten-cow spreads in the Hole, but nobody was willing to sell, Laura Bailey least of all.

Laura was given to hunches, but Dan didn't know why she'd had this one about not having long to live. There was no reason for it.

Nobody, not even Justin Albright, went around shooting women, but Dan was very much aware that Laura was unable to be rational about it.

Bald Rock sat on a bench above the river. A plank bridge spanned the stream at this point, connecting the ranches on the west side of Green river with those on the east. The settlement wasn't big enough to be called a town, but everyone in the Hole referred to it as 'town' because the only post office, store, and saloon in the Hole were located here. This one log structure, along with the white frame school building and the cabin back of the schoolhouse which was the teacherage, made up the settlement.

Dan dismounted in front of the store at the end of the long line of horses and tied. As he stepped onto the porch, Bess Bailey came through the door. She was smiling at him, or seemed to be smiling. A second glance told him it was more of a triumphant smirk than a smile. She nodded at the teacherage, saying, 'What are you going to do about it, Mr. Matson?'

Bess had a talent for making every hair on the back of his neck stand out like the quills on a porcupine and not use more than ten words to accomplish it. It was her tone as much as her words that did it. He said, 'Now why does Queen Bess want to know what I'm going to do about what?'

It made her just as furious to be called 'Queen Bess.' Her face turned red, and for a moment he thought she was going to hit him with her fist. Sometimes she did, and being a strong woman, she packed quite a punch. When she tried, they always wound up in a wrestling match with Dan eventually the winner, but today she wasn't in the mood for it and she held her temper.

She nodded at the teacherage again. 'What are you going to do about Lee Jackson? I understood you told him to stay out of the Hole and let your girl alone.'

He wheeled to stare at the teacherage, noticing for the first time that Jackson's big sorrel was tied in front of Margo Lane's cabin. He said in a low voice, 'I don't claim Margo as my girl and you damned well know it. What I told Jackson was that I'd bust his back if he showed his face in the Hole again and I'll do it.'

'Now that should be quite a show,' she murmured. 'I want to see you do it.' She turned away, then swung back. 'The next thing I know you'll be promising to paddle my little ass until I can't sit down for a week. That will be quite a show, too.'

This time she did turn with a flip of her hips and stalked into the store.

CHAPTER TWO

Lee Jackson reined his sorrel gelding to a stop when he reached the mouth of Maroon creek canyon, his gaze sweeping Smith's Hole that lay in front of him. He could not see all of it from here because it stretched far to the north. A number of rocky ridges running from the eastern bluffs to the river blocked his view, but he could see that most of the grass was knee-high on a horse, more grass than the Hole ranchers could possibly need for their small herds.

There was, of course, the other side to the coin. If the Skull steer herd poured down Maroon creek and wintered in the Hole, there would be nothing left by late spring except the grass that was fenced in, the quarter sections that had been proved up on by the local ranchers and were largely used to raise hay or grain. There were exceptions, pastures holding the milk cows that were kept on some of the ranches, but they were too small to be of much practical use.

Jackson touched his horse up and rode on slowly toward Bald Rock, thinking as he had so many times since Justin Albright had stated his intention of using the Hole for winter graze that blood would be spilled before Albright achieved his goal. Jackson was by nature a

10

peaceful man, and working for Justin Albright was both dangerous and difficult and not a proper job for him.

The danger could be faced. The difficult part came in swallowing his pride and ignoring his conscience. He had almost reached the point where he could not go on. It was, he thought grimly, a good deal like riding a bad horse. It was tough to stay on, but hell to get off.

Even riding alone into Smith's Hole was dangerous, but bringing Skull riders with him would have been an admission of fear, and he would never give Dan Matson that much satisfaction. He wasn't afraid of Matson, but he was afraid that the Hole men would gang up on him. They hated Albright so much that they might beat Lee Jackson to death because he represented Skull, and they knew they would never get a crack at Albright himself.

Jackson had three reasons for coming. Any one of the three would have been enough to have brought him here. The first was to check on the grass and to warn the Hole ranchers again that within the next two or three weeks the Skull herd would be here. Those who wanted to sell and get a fair price had better do it now before the Skull steers were driven down Maroon creek. Justin Albright was hard on men who bucked him. The second reason was strictly personal. Dan Matson had warned him the last time he'd been here to stay out of

11

the Hole, and Jackson was not one to ignore such a challenge. The third reason was tied in with the second. He wanted to see Margo Lane. He hated Matson because the Hole man was a rival, and Matson had an edge because he lived here and could see Margo anytime.

He reached the schoolhouse and reined up in front and tied, noting the line of horses in front of Charley Klein's store and saloon. They were waiting for him, he thought sourly as he walked to the teacherage. He'd expected it. This was Saturday, the day when most ranchers went to town. Besides, they were aware that their time was running out.

As far as he knew, they had not reached an agreement about selling. Probably they were making their decision now. Well, he'd go to the store after visiting with Margo, and then, he thought ruefully, all hell would break loose and fall on him before he could get out of the Hole.

Margo saw him before he reached the teacherage. She jerked the door open and came flying across the porch to fall into his arms, crying, 'Lee! Oh Lee, it's so good to see you.'

He hugged her, thinking that she must love him, that she could not act out a lie so convincingly, and yet he had never been sure of her love. She liked men, she liked their adulation, and he could not escape the depressing feeling that she greeted Dan

Matson with the same enthusiasm with which she had just greeted him.

For a moment he pushed her away and stared down at her blue eyes that seemed so full of love for him. Then he kissed her, and he could no longer doubt her love. She proved it in the way she clung to him, in the way her passionate lips and tongue were torches fanning his desire. She set him on fire as no other woman had ever done; he wanted to pick her up and carry her into her bedroom, drop her on the bed and tear the clothes off her tiny, sensuous body.

As much as he wanted this, he could not do it, although he often had the feeling she hungered for it as much as he did. She was so small, so defenseless. She was less than five feet tall, she weighed no more than one hundred pounds, and when he was with her, he always felt like a great hulking giant.

She reminded him of a fragile toy, or perhaps a bird that could easily be injured by his strong hands. He guessed this was part of what held him back. He was afraid he would hurt her, and he could never have forgiven himself if he had.

She shivered in his arms. 'Come in out of the sun, Lee.' She shivered again and tugged at his hands. 'You don't know what you do to me, Lee. I was perfectly all right until you kissed me, and now . . .'

She left the sentence unfinished. He

13

followed her into the house, saying, 'Did you ever think about what you do to me, Margo?'

She whirled to face him, her skirt flying away from her ankles. 'It makes me happy to hear that,' she whispered. 'Sometimes I think it's one-sided. I love you so much, Lee.'

'When are we getting married?' he asked.

She sighed. 'Sit down, Lee. I was just getting dinner. We can fix some more sandwiches. There's plenty of coffee. I made a custard pie this morning. I didn't know why I did, but now I do. It was because you were coming.'

She brought bread and butter and part of a cold roast from the pantry. He said, 'I asked you a question. You ain't getting out of it by appealing to my stomach.'

She laughed. He liked to hear her laugh It was always a free, wild sound that made him realize there was a part of her he didn't know, an untamed part that was beyond his touch. Perhaps it was this part of her that made him instinctively distrust her. Then he decided he didn't really like to hear her laughter because he wanted to trust her, wanted to be sure of her love.

'I'll tell you when I'll marry you,' she said. 'When you can give me a house to live in. I won't live in your cow camp. I wouldn't trust your woman-hungry men.'

'No, I guess that wouldn't be any place for you to live,' he admitted. 'I've been thinking about it since I was here the last time. I don't

14

want to keep putting off our marriage. I know I'll lose you if I do and I can't bear to even think of that, so I've made up my mind that this will be my last year working for Albright. I'm going to buy that little spread on the Michigan in North Park we've talked about. You remember we went fishing there one time. It ain't a big outfit, but we can make a living on it and there's a purty good house we can fix . . .'

'And just when will you buy it?' she demanded.

'As soon as we settle this business about wintering the Skull herd in Smith's Hole,' he said. 'I've got enough money in the bank in Laramie to handle it. I'll ride over to North Park and make an offer just as soon as . . .'

She straightened up and looked at him from the end of the table where she had been slicing bread. 'Lee Jackson, you're a slave to old Justin Albright, and I'll never believe that you will actually quit working for him until I know you've done it.'

'Damn it, Margo, if I promise you . . .'

'And another thing,' she went on. 'They'll kill you if you keep working for Albright. Do you think for a minute that Dan Matson or Nate Willets or Lige Carter will let you steal their grass?'

'Nobody stops Skull,' he said harshly. 'You know that. Sure, there'll be a fight, but Justin Albright will send an army in here if he has to,

15

and Judge Verling will see to it that the law don't interfere.'

She stamped her foot. 'Oh, how can you be so blind. Sure, Verling will do what he can, but Sheriff Douglas won't stand still for murder, and that's what it'll be if Albright gives you an army to clear everybody out.'

'Douglas can't do much if Verling won't sentence the men that Douglas brings in. It's the legal end that counts. How do you think Albright has made his money? By conniving with men like Judge Verling. That's how.'

'And that makes you as dishonest as old Albright is,' she said.

'No, it don't,' he said. 'I carry out orders. That's all. I never done no conniving.'

'Lee, you don't know these men the way I do,' she said angrily. 'I live here and I hear them talk. It won't make any difference how many men Albright sends into the Hole. Until you get Matson and Willets and Carter out of the way, you'll never get the Hole grass for Skull. They'll die, maybe, but they won't give up until they are dead, and they'll do a lot of killing before you kill them.'

He shifted his weight uneasily in his chair, realizing that she was saying what he'd been thinking all the time. He had been fooling himself by trying to ignore it just as Justin Albright did. The old man had been used to having his way, going on the assumption that he could browbeat those who stood in his way

16

or buy anything he wanted.

She started to slice the roast, saying, 'You go ahead and eat, Lee. Make your sandwich the way you want it. I'll get the coffee and bring in the pie.'

He ate in silence, a sense of uneasiness gripping him. He couldn't risk losing Margo, but he couldn't quit his job with Albright, either, not with a fight looming ahead the way it was. Everyone would think he'd quit because he was afraid.

Damn it, he told himself angrily, he was afraid, and that was the reason he couldn't quit. He didn't want anyone to know or even suspect. He was afraid to go into the store, but that was something else he had to do. Maybe it was pride that drove him, or the need to keep his self-respect. Or maybe it was a matter of proving to himself that he could do something he was afraid to do.

When he finished eating, he scooted his chair back and rose. 'I've got to go to the store and remind them they've only got a couple of weeks to sell and move out.'

She jumped up and ran around the table to him. She gripped his arms and tried to shake them. 'No, Lee,' she cried. 'No. They'll kill you. Can't you understand that? I want a live husband. A dead man won't do me any good.'

'I've got to go,' he said. 'That's something you ought to understand. I've loved you ever since the winter you taught school in North

17

Park and I rode through them damned storms to see you on Sunday afternoons. Don't forget that, Margo. Don't ever forget it, and don't forget that there's some things a man has to do even if he don't want to.'

She stepped away from him, her face turning stony. He left the room, a big young man who had suddenly become an old and lumbering man who realized he may have thrown his future away and did not know what to do about it.

CHAPTER THREE

Dan Matson went into Klein's store behind Bess, saw that no one was there, and followed her into the saloon. He glanced around and nodded his greeting, noting that every rancher in the Hole was present. They had been waiting for him and he sensed their impatience.

He stopped at the bar. He said, 'Whiskey.'

Charley Klein had been standing next to a window. Nodding, he hobbled behind the bar and poured Dan's drink. He was an old man as withered as the last apple hanging on a tree in spring. He'd come to the Hole shortly after Al Bailey had. He'd ranched, then after he'd been crippled up breaking horses, he'd bought a store and saloon that another man had started.

Dan didn't know how old Charley was, but he'd been middle-aged when he'd come to the Hole, a much older man than Al Bailey had been, so he was probably in his eighties. He was still sound mentally, he could see and hear as well as any man, and he hated Justin Albright with more passion than anyone else in the Hole.

'I've seen 'em come and go,' he'd said more than once. 'Greedy devils who use the law and their power to take anything they want, bastards like Albright who hire other men to do their dirty work. I came here to get away from men like that, and now by God I'm too old to run again.'

Dan knew Klein could be counted on to stay till the finish. So could Willets and Carter. Bess, of course. Beyond that Dan wasn't sure of any man in the room except Buffalo Jack Roman who owned Hatchet on the other side of the river. Roman, too, had been one of the first settlers. He was about Laura Bailey's age, probably in his late fifties, a bachelor who had asked Laura to many him a dozen times and still had hopes that sometime she would say yes.

Bess had moved to the bar to stand beside Dan. She said, 'I'll have whiskey, too, Charley.'

Dan wheeled to face her. She'd done this before and it always made him furious. It did now. He glared at her, wanting to grab the whiskey glass out of her hand. He'd done that

19

once and she'd swarmed over him like a she-bear with cubs. Now she ignored him as she gulped her drink.

There was nothing he could do, he told himself, unless he wanted to start another fight and that was the last thing he wanted this morning. He glanced at the men in the room sitting at the green-topped tables or in chairs along the wall.

Big Lige Carter with the usual half-smoked cigarette hanging to his lower lip. Slender Nate Willets with the .45 tied down on his right thigh. Raw-boned Buffalo Jack Roman with a half-smile on his face as if he found Bess's man-playing amusing. The rest of them waiting, expectant, impatient.

'Go on home to your ma,' Dan said in a low tone. 'She needs you.'

'She'll be there when we get done here,' Bess said, taking the makings from her shirt pocket and rolling a smoke.

She was even dressed like a man, in a work shirt and Levis and high-heeled boots. Her hair was cut almost as short as a man's, and if it hadn't been for the swell of her breasts and buttocks, she could be taken for a man.

Dan fought his temper, not sure whether she was baiting him, which he always suspected to be the case, or whether she actually felt more at ease playing this game which she had played since her father's death. He habitually responded with a cold and vindictive fury,

20

which may have been exactly what she wanted. Now he turned away from her, leaving his drink untasted on the bar.

'Bess tell you boys what she and her ma found in their barn this morning?' Dan asked.

'Yeah, she done that,' Jack Roman answered. 'How do you figure it, Dan? Maybe Buck Douglas will be showing up purty soon looking for that hide?'

'That's about the size of it,' Dan agreed. 'I'm riding up Maroon creek figuring on meeting him and telling him what he'll find. I don't think he'll push it.'

'I don't want no God-damned sheriff poking around here,' Nate Willets growled. 'That's what I came here to get away from.'

'Me, too,' Lige Carter said in his slow drawl. 'I never feel good when I see one of them nice, shiny stars on a man's shirt. Maybe we just oughtta string him up and stretch his neck an inch or two.'

Neither man had made any attempt to hide the fact that he had ridden out of Texas one jump ahead of the law, but neither had ever said what he had done to get the law on his trail. The Hole people had accepted them for what they were, and both men had felt at home from the day they had appeared here. Now Dan studied first Willets and then Carter, knowing that this was a test of sorts.

'No, Lige,' Dan said mildly. 'I figure the sheriff is our friend. It's my guess he don't like

Skull no more than we do. If we rough him up, we'll just make more trouble. We've got enough now.'

'That's right,' Jack Roman agreed.

'He ain't taking me to no stinking jail in Craig,' Willets muttered. 'He ain't taking Laura Bailey, either.'

Carter nodded as he tossed his cigarette stub into the nearest spittoon and started to roll another. 'We ain't had no law man in the Hole since we came. I don't like having one now. I dunno if he gets reward dodgers from Texas or not, but if he does, and if he recognizes me, we're in for more trouble whether you want it or not. Leastwise me 'n' Nate are.'

'Stay out of his sight,' Dan said. 'I don't figure he's gonna be looking for anything except that hide and I aim to set him straight on that. We need Buck on our side I think we can play him against Judge Verling.'

'One thing's sure,' Roman said. 'Verling can't give us no jail sentence if Douglas don't bring us in. Maybe he won't try taking any of us in if we don't give him no trouble.'

'That's all right for you to say,' Willets snapped, his thin face reflecting his fear, 'but I've got a price on my head dead or alive. I don't figure Buck Douglas or no other badge toter is gonna pass that up if he knows it.'

Bess finished her cigarette and tossed the stub into a spittoon. She said, 'Nate, you know

22

we're your friends, don't you?'

'Sure, but . . .'

'Now hold on,' Bess broke in. 'You likewise know that if it comes to taking you to Craig, Buck will have to deal with all of us, just as we know that if Albright sends an army of Skull riders into the Hole, we can count on you and Lige siding us.'

'Yeah, I know that, too,' Willets agreed.

'You too, Lige?'

'Hell, yes,' Carter said.

'All right, then,' Bess said. 'It gravels the hell out of me to agree with my neighbor, Mr. Matson, but he's right about staying out of the sheriff's sight. Buck knows as well as you do that he can't take anybody out of Smith's Hole without a posse, and he'd have trouble then. If he did aim to take one of you, he'd bring a posse with him. We'll start worrying about you when he does.'

Both men relaxed, Willets saying, 'Well now, Miss Bess, that does make sense. It's just that we don't want to stir up no trouble for you folks.'

'We've got trouble whether you and Lige do any stirring or not,' Jack Roman said grimly. 'We called this meeting to decide what to do when Albright sends his herd into the Hole. So far I ain't heard no talking about it.'

'I say we draw lots,' Bess said, 'and make up a schedule for keeping two men on Maroon creek to hold 'em back while we get word to everybody about what's going on. If we're all there in the canyon, we can keep 'em out of the Hole.'

Charley Klein came around the end of the bar to stand beside Bess. 'That's right. By grab, she's the best man of the lot of you. You've got to fight 'em. Powdersmoke is the only thing a man like Justin Albright understands.'

The men nodded. One of them said slowly, 'I sure don't hanker to get shot, but me 'n' my family have got a living here the way things stand now. One winter of having a Skull herd in the Hole means that we don't have no grass left. That means no cattle after this winter and that means no living for me and my wife and my kids.'

'It's as simple as that,' another man agreed. 'We've lived together in the Hole for nigh onto twenty years, getting along with each other and all of us making a living. We ain't got room for Justin Albright.'

'Some of us have lived here more 'n twenty years,' Klein said bitterly. 'I'm staying and I'm fighting. I've run before and I can tell you a man don't feel good when he does. You're better off dead.'

'Oh hell,' Dan exploded. 'What's the matter with you, Charley? Nobody's talking about running.'

'Well now,' the old man sputtered, 'it strikes me I've been hearing a lot of soft talk ever since Albright sent word that he was driving

24

his steer herd into the Hole. Well sir, he ain't running me out of here. I'm gonna die in my bed and Justin Albright ain't—'

'All right, all right,' Dan broke in. 'We'll help you die wherever you want to. What we're here for is to decide the best way to fight Skull. You all know damned well that we can't keep two men on Maroon creek day after day, and you likewise know that if we did, two men couldn't keep the Skull herd out of the Hole.'

'Maybe you've got a better notion,' Bess snapped.

'Maybe I have,' Dan said hotly. 'We'll build a log pile on top of Lone Rock and we'll keep one man up there to touch off a fire when he sees the herd moving this way. I say let 'em come into the Hole. While they're coming, we'll see the fire and get together here at the store.

'I don't know how many men they'll have, but we've got enough to shoot hell out of 'em. Right now I say to do nothing until we've talked to Douglas. I also say to get word to Lee Jackson about what we'll do. We'll tell him to pass the word to Albright. I don't figure we'll change the old bastard's mind, but we might change his men's minds if they know what they're heading into.'

'I'm willing to go to their cow camp and tell 'em personally,' Willets said. 'Me 'n' Lige have scared off bigger outfits than Skull.' He patted his holstered gun. 'This is our kind of game. If

25

any of the Skull riders jump us, we'll take care of 'em.'

'Speaking of Lee Jackson,' Bess said with satisfaction, 'you can tell him right now, Mr. Matson. Likewise we'll see what you're gonna do about keeping your word, which was to bust his back if he showed his face in Smith's Hole again.'

Dan wheeled toward the nearest window. Lee Jackson was tying his horse in front of the store.

CHAPTER FOUR

Lee Jackson stepped up on the porch of Charley Klein's store building, then hesitated. At that moment he was very close to turning back to his horse and riding out of Smith's Hole. Let Justin Albright bring his own messages, he thought. If he went inside, he'd be lucky to get out alive. Then he remembered Dan Matson's threat. He could not overlook a challenge as direct as that, so he went on through the south door into the saloon.

He said, 'Howdy,' and glanced around the room.

He didn't know all of the Hole ranchers by name, but he knew their faces and he knew how many there were. He didn't count the men who were here, but he guessed that none

26

were missing. Then he noticed Bess Bailey standing at the bar beside Matson. In that first quick glance he had mistaken her for a man.

Some of them nodded, but most of them did not speak or greet him in any way. He felt their hostile eyes on him, challenging him, inviting him to start trouble, hating him because to them he was Skull.

Jackson's right hand was close to his gun butt as he saw Lige Carter move slowly toward him, his broad face impassive. He showed the least feeling of any man in the room, but Jackson knew him well enough to realize that he hid his feelings, that he would fight for his small holding in Smith's Hole as hard as any of them.

'Stop where you are, Carter,' Jackson said. 'I sure ain't asking for trouble, or I'd have brought my crew with me. I came to tell you that the Skull herd will be here in about two weeks. Mr. Albright ordered me to tell you he'll buy any of you out for a fair price. In other words, you name what you think your spread's worth and he'll give it to you if it's within reason. If you wait until the herd is here, he won't . . .'

'You think your threats are going to make us run?' old Charley Klein squealed. 'By God, you're barking up the wrong tree. You go back and tell that bastard . . .'

'Hold on, Charley,' Bess Bailey said. 'Let's have Jackson tell us what right Albright has to steal our grass.'

'He ain't figuring on stealing your grass,' Jackson said, backing up so that he was against the wall. His right hand was still close to his gun butt as his gaze swept the room. 'Whatever you have fenced is your land and we won't bother it. What we're taking is the public domain. Mr. Albright has as much right to it as anyone. It ain't yours just because you've been using it all this time. If you want to turn your cattle loose to mix with our herd, that's up to you, but some of 'em may disappear come spring when we leave the Hole.'

Lige Carter had edged closer to him. Jackson had not caught him making a move, but he had a fluid grace that enabled him to move like a cat. Jackson said angrily, 'Damn it, Carter, I don't want no trouble, so stay where you are. I've said my piece, and now I'm sloping out of here.'

Dan Matson laughed. 'I don't think so, Jackson. You asked for trouble the minute you walked through that door. I'm going to beat hell out of you like I told you I would if you ever showed your ugly mug around here again.'

'I ain't gonna fight you,' Jackson shouted. 'All I aimed to do was to give you Albright's message.'

His hand gripped the butt of his gun. Matson said, 'We've heard that message before. We figure it's mostly bluff. If it ain't, you tell Albright he's gonna see more hot lead than he's ever seen in his life if the Skull herd comes out of Maroon canyon into the Hole. Now shuck your gun belt.'

Matson turned and, unbuckling his gun belt, laid it on the bar. Jackson's gun was half out of leather when Carter said in his soft drawl, 'You're fighting him, all right. Now shove it back and unbuckle your belt and drop it.'

Jackson froze, his gaze coming once more to the black man. Carter's gun was in his hand. He was standing no more than ten feet away. How he had eased up that last fifteen feet and pulled his gun without Jackson being aware of his movement was more than he could understand, but Carter was there, all right. Jackson was as sure as he could be sure of anything that if he didn't drop his gun belt Carter would kill him.

It would be murder, but Buck Douglas wouldn't hear the story that way. Even if the sheriff guessed the truth, he'd never get Carter or any other Hole man out of here. They'd hang tight, and that made him a fool for coming.

Slowly Jackson eased his gun back into the holster, then loosened the latch and dropped the belt to the floor. He asked, 'You fixing to steal my gun and belt, Matson?'

'You'll get 'em when you leave,' Matson said.

For just a moment everyone in the room

29

seemed frozen. There was no sound except the labored breathing of a dozen men sawing into the quiet, then a rooster crowed from somewhere behind the saloon, the sound inordinately loud. Suddenly Dan Matson was on him, his fists swinging.

Jackson drove a hard right into Matson's face, the blow sending the Hole man back on his heels. Jackson was twenty pounds heavier and he had the advantage of two or three inches of reach. It occurred to him that he had nothing to worry about. He could whip Matson, pick up his gun belt, and walk out of here. Then he'd be done with the whole damned business.

He charged Matson, his right swinging again at the Hole man's head, but the head wasn't there. Matson ducked and for a moment Jackson was off balance and defenseless. Matson hit him with one fist and then the other, pile-driving blows that slammed his head back and forth like a ball on a string. The next thing he knew he was on the floor. He started to get up, but he couldn't make it.

He tried again and this time he struggled to his hands and knees, but that was the best he could do. Matson stood over him, his fists cocked. From a great distance, it seemed, Matson's words came to him, 'Why did you plant that Skull hide in Laura Bailey's barn?'

Skull hide? He didn't know anything about a Skull hide. He must not have heard right.

Matson wasn't standing still. No, that wasn't it. There were two Matsons. Twins! One was the real Matson, but he couldn't tell which was which.

He started to say he didn't know anything about a Skull hide when Lige Carter said, 'Dan, I ain't et a man's liver for a long time. I wonder if this bastard's liver is worth cutting out of him?'

'Hell no,' another man said. 'Let's cut his heart out and send it to Albright.'

By God, he thought, they'd do it. He forced himself to his feet, blood streaming down his chin from his nose. The two Matsons were directly in front of him. Jackson tried again, his right fist slamming squarely at one of their heads, but he must have tried for the wrong head. He hit nothing more solid than air. The next instant Matson's right fist caught his chin in a sledging blow that knocked him down.

'I'll ask you once more,' Matson said. 'If you don't answer me, I'll turn these liver and heart hungry men loose on you with their knives. Why did you plant that hide in Laura Bailey's barn?'

'I . . . didn't . . . plant . . . no . . . hide,' Jackson muttered, his head lifting and falling back to the floor.

'He's lying,' a woman said harshly.

'I ain't so sure,' Matson said. 'Pick him up. Got a room where we can leave him, Charley?'

'Sure,' Charley Klein said. 'Fetch him

31

along.'

Jackson was vaguely aware of being lifted and carried the length of the saloon. He heard someone ask, 'You gonna hang him now or later, Dan?'

'We ain't gonna hang him,' Matson said sharply. 'I'll take care of anybody who bothers him while I'm gone. I figure Buck Douglas will want to ask him some questions, then we'll turn him loose.'

'I'll bet he won't be bothering your girl no more,' a woman said.

'You're making a mistake,' a man said. 'You oughtta hang him That'd teach Albright a lesson.'

'No,' Matson said angrily. 'You do that and we'll be the ones who'll be hanging. There's no sense in cutting off a limb when it's the root we want. Justin Albright is the root and until we get him, we'll have trouble.'

They dropped him on a bed and left, the woman still grumbling that she figured he knew about that hide. They closed the door behind them. For a long time Jackson didn't move. He stared at the ceiling, his bandanna wadded up into a ball of cloth. He pressed it against his nose, but still the blood dripped. He'd done his share of fighting, but he'd never been whipped as quickly or completely as Dan Matson had whipped him today.

Slowly his head cleared. Apparently he was in Charley Klein's bedroom. The bed was a foul-smelling one that made him wonder how the old man could stand it. There was only one window and it was closed. It was so small that there could be no escape through it.

He got up, swaying uncertainly, and tried the door. It was heavy and solid and refused to give an inch. No lock or latch. Apparently there was a turn pin on the other side and they had given it a twist when they'd left so that the door was tightly locked. He could not escape. He was right here until they decided to let him loose. If they did, he thought grudgingly, it would be because Dan Matson said to.

He lay down again, his mind going back to what the woman . . . that would be Bess Bailey . . . had said about him staying away from Matson's girl. That would have to be Margo Lane. The thought made him even sicker than Matson's pounding. He had known that Matson was shining around Margo, but for them to call her Matson's girl was too much. Then he felt better as the thought occurred to him it was Matson's idea, not Margo's. Well, he'd have it out with her the next time he saw her. If she wasn't his girl, he'd better be knowing it now.

His nose had stopped bleeding, but his head still hurt from the beating he had taken. Matson's blows had had the power of mule kicks. He closed his eyes and tried to think. Matson had asked about a Skull hide and Bess Bailey had not believed him when he'd told

Matson he knew nothing about it. It made no sense. He had never planted a hide on anyone.

Hours later, or so it seemed, Bess Bailey opened the door and brought him a plate of food. She said, 'Sit up, Jackson. We don't want you starving to death or you telling the sheriff we abused you.'

He wasn't hungry. All he wanted was to get out of here. He sat up, staring at the Bailey woman, then got to his feet and lunged past her toward the open door. Just as he reached it, Lige Carter appeared, his big body barring the passage. Carter put his hands out and gave Jackson a shove with his open palms. Jackson went back a good ten feet and sprawled on the floor.

'Oh, I don't think you'd better leave,' the Bailey woman said. 'I'll put your dinner on the bureau. You can eat it or go hungry. It's nothing to me either way.'

'You ready to tell us about that Skull hide?' Carter demanded.

'I don't know nothing about no hide,' Jackson muttered. 'I told you that.'

'Maybe he don't,' Bess Bailey said. 'Dan said it didn't seem like a sneaky thing he'd do. Maybe Albright got somebody else to do it.'

'Naw, he's lying,' Carter said contemptuously. 'Who else would do it? If it was me running things, I'd stretch his neck a little and he'd remember quick enough.'

They went out, closing the door behind

them. He yelled, 'How long you gonna keep me locked up?'

Neither answered. He got up and sat on the edge of the bed. His nose started to bleed again. He pressed his bandanna against it. After it stopped, he got up and tried to drink the coffee. It was worse than tar. He looked at the ham and the two fried eggs that stared back at him like two rheumy, orange eyes. He turned and fell across the bed.

He thought about the hide they kept asking about. He knew he still wasn't thinking straight, but he was dead sure he'd had nothing to do with planting a hide on Laura Bailey or anyone else. So, if they were telling the truth, Justin Albright had hired someone in the Skull crew to butcher a steer and plant the hide on Laura Bailey's property. That meant Albright was working around Lee Jackson.

The hell of it was no one would believe him. He'd be held responsible for anything that happened whether he'd had any responsibility for it or not. If it came to murder, and it could, well, he wasn't going to swing for Justin Albright or anyone else.

CHAPTER FIVE

Dan Matson reined up in front of Margo Lane's cabin, dismounted, and tied. He knew he should keep on riding to meet Buck Douglas, but he wanted to know what had been said when Jackson had stopped here. Besides, he just plain wanted to see Margo. It had been a week since he'd talked to her and that seemed a long time.

Still, he refused to admit even to himself that she was his girl and he resented the way Bess Bailey kept throwing it up to him. Margo was attractive, she liked him, and maybe, just maybe, she'd make a good rancher's wife. The trouble was she was flighty, perhaps too flighty to settle down, but once she was actually married, she might stop flirting with every man who came along.

Dan knew that his real problem was his own feeling for Margo. When he was with her, he usually forgot his doubts and questions. She had a way of making him think she was crazy in love with him. The trouble was she had a magnetic power that drew men to her. That was the basis of his doubts.

He'd had more than one fight because other men had been too attentive to her at dances or parties. She enjoyed being fought over. That as much as anything got under his hide. One

36

thing was sure. He didn't want a wife who constantly created situations which forced a fight on him every time he took her anywhere. The truth was he'd never convinced himself that she would change once she had recited the marriage vows.

Today was no different from other days when he had stopped to see her. She met him before he reached her front door and threw herself into his arms, crying, 'Oh, Dan, where have you been all week?'

'Home,' he said. 'Working.'

She kissed him. She never withheld her kisses, never gave him any reason to doubt her love for him, but even now as he held her soft body in his arms and responded to her urgent kiss, he could not forget that Lee Jackson had been with her only an hour ago.

He pushed her back and looked down at her. Her moist red lips were slightly parted, her blue eyes wide with questions. 'What's the matter, Dan?' she whispered. 'Are you mad at me?'

'No, of course not.'

She reached up and tenderly touched the bruise on the side of his face where Jackson had hit him. 'What happened to you?'

'I had a fight with your friend Jackson,' Dan said. 'He got in one good lick before I whipped him.'

'He's bigger than you are,' she said softly. 'I was afraid he'd whip you, but I'm glad he didn't.' She sighed and shook her head. 'But how many times have I told you not to fight over me.'

'We didn't fight over you,' he said quickly, thinking how typical of her to assume that they had. 'I'd told him to stay out of the Hole, but he came in anyhow with another warning from Albright, so I had to show him that it wasn't healthy for a Skull man to show his face around here. We don't want no more threats from Justin Albright.'

'I'm glad I wasn't the cause of your fight,' she said. 'Come in. I'll pour you a cup of coffee. Maybe you'd like a piece of pie.'

'No pie,' he said, 'but I'll take the coffee.'

He followed her into the cabin, suspecting that she was disappointed because the fight wasn't over her, then he was ashamed of the thought. He watched her walk to the stove and pour the coffee, admiring the way she moved, the soft curves of her breasts and hips, the way she had of never letting him forget that she was a woman. He wondered bitterly why Bess Bailey couldn't have just a little of Margo Lane's femininity which she possessed in such abundance.

'Sit down, Dan,' she said as she brought the coffee to him. 'I know you've been busy, but I did hope you'd ride over some evening. School will be starting in a couple of weeks and then I'll be busy, but I've got plenty of time to visit now and I get lonesome for you.'

38

He sat down and sipped his coffee. She returned to the stove and poured a cup for herself. He watched her, uneasy for some reason. Maybe it was because he kept remembering that Lee Jackson had been here for a long time. Margo must have made him welcome or he wouldn't have stayed so long. But how welcome? Again he was ashamed of his thoughts about her.

Still, he could not drive the ugly picture from his mind. In spite of himself, he asked, 'What did you and Jackson talk about?'

'Well now,' she said tartly, 'I don't know that it's any of your business. You can't hold a claim you haven't staked out, you know.'

'Maybe Jackson's staked out the claim,' he said.

She tossed her head defiantly. 'Now maybe he has. Would it make any difference to you if he had?'

'You know damned well it would,' he snapped, 'but right now that ain't the point. A showdown is coming with Skull in a few days. I've got a right to know what's going on between you and him.'

'Oh no, you haven't,' she said. 'What goes on between Lee and me has nothing to do with your showdown with Skull.'

'It would if he tells you anything about Albright's plans,' Dan insisted.

'I don't know anything about Albright's plans. You must be crazy. Why would Lee tell

39

me about them?'

'I don't know,' Dan shouted angrily. 'Damn it, I'm just trying to find out.'

'You forget that Lee and I have been friends for a long time,' she said. 'I taught school one term in North Park before I came here. Lee was there that winter. He came to see me then, and if he wants to come and see me here, it's our business, not yours. You haven't exactly worn a path to my front door, Mr. Matson.'

He banged his cup on the table as he set it down. 'I can't be riding over here every evening this time of year and you know it. You know something else? Jackson's coming here has a lot to do with our showdown. Maybe he didn't really come to see you. Maybe he used it as an excuse to spy on us. All I know is that we're in a fight for our lives and you're welcoming the enemy.'

'He's not my enemy,' she flung at him. 'I'm not in your old fight and I'm not going to be. Maybe you'd better get something straight right now. If you want to marry me, you're going to have to say so. You come around and ask me to go to dances with you, or you just sit and drink my coffee and act like you enjoy my company, but I don't know what's in your mind or even what your intentions are. I'll tell you one thing. Lee Jackson wants to marry me. I think I'll say yes and let him take me out of this miserable hole in the ground.'

'And leave us without a teacher for next

winter?' He shook his head. 'No, I think you'll wait till spring.'

He finished his coffee, his uneasiness growing. He knew now what he had suspected, that Jackson wanted to marry Margo and she hadn't said no. She was dangling both of them and enjoying it. The thought made him furious.

These were the first hard words that had ever passed between them. He didn't want to leave this way, but he didn't like the way she was playing both ends against the middle. Again in spite of himself, he said harshly, 'Go ahead and marry Jackson if that's what you want. You know as well as I do that I hope to marry you, but I won't do it as long as we're having trouble with Skull. I wouldn't marry any woman just to make a widow out of her.'

She ran to him and hugged him. 'That's what I wanted to hear, Dan. You never said before that you wanted to many me. You've never even told me that you loved me. How was I to know how you felt?'

He'd done it now, he thought glumly. He'd fallen into her trap and that was what he'd been trying to avoid. He tipped his head to kiss her expectant lips, then wheeled away, saying, 'I've got to ride. I've been here too long now.'

He strode to the door, her words coming to him, 'Let's not wait, Dan. I know you'll work this out without a lot of killing.'

He glanced back; he saw an expression of

41

satisfaction on her face, and for a moment he actually hated her for trapping him. He said, 'So long,' and, striding rapidly to his horse, mounted and rode away.

He did not look back at her again, but he kept seeing her face with that smug expression of satisfaction. She was happy now, he thought sourly. She had two men dancing on the same string. Maybe when it got right down to cases, she wouldn't marry either one. It was too much fun to keep them dangling.

CHAPTER SIX

Minutes after he left Margo Lane, Dan was in Maroon canyon, the red-rock cliffs rising two hundred feet or more on both sides of him. The lower part of the sides of the walls were so sheer that no human being could climb them, but near the top the slick rock rims sloped back for another two hundred feet.

About a mile from the mouth of the canyon he passed Lone Rock, a steep sandstone peak on his left. This was the high point where he had said they could build a signal fire and post a sentry twenty-four hours a day to notify the Hole people if the Skull herd was being driven toward them.

The top of Lone Rock was high enough so that a man stationed there could see for miles across the sagebrush desert to the east. He would observe dust raised by the herd long before the cattle actually came into sight. It would give the Hole men at least half a day to reach the mouth of Maroon canyon from their homes.

The steep walls of the canyon held for about a mile, then they dropped off, making a slope so gradual that a man and horse would have no trouble climbing to the top. Another mile brought him completely out of the canyon. From here the rolling sage-covered hills stretched as far as he could see to the east and south. He could make out the line of green that marked the course of the Little Snake. Out there somewhere was the Skull herd, slowly being pushed toward Smith's Hole.

The road was a narrow, twin-rutted ribbon through the sagebrush, branching about three miles to the east, one fork angling south toward Craig, the other north toward Baggs or the Wyoming-Colorado line.

Dan reined up and studied the horizon. If he had guessed right, Buck Douglas should be in sight. A moment later he sighed in relief when he made out a lone rider coming in on the Craig road. Dan put his horse into a gallop, suddenly anxious to have this meeting over with.

Then he pulled the gelding down to a slower pace, realizing he was letting his nerves push him too hard. This meeting with the sheriff was important, so important that the entire outcome of the fight with Skull might swing on what the sheriff did today.

Dan did not know Buck Douglas well. As a matter of fact, no one in Smith's Hole knew anyone in Craig well. Not in the tight bonds of friendship that marked the relationship of the people in the Hole. The only reason the Smith's Hole people had for going to Craig was to buy supplies or attend to county business, and no one in Craig ever came to the Hole, except the doctor if a case was urgent or a preacher to hold services in the schoolhouse.

Smith's Hole was a tight little community, sufficient unto itself for all practical purposes. The one thing its people wanted was to be let alone. Dan was sure that Buck Douglas understood this.

Until he was elected sheriff, Douglas had been a small rancher in the southern part of Moffat county, and he certainly shared the feeling that the Smith's Hole people had toward a big cowman like Justin Albright. The question in Dan's mind was whether Albright had been able to buy Douglas as he had unquestionably bought Judge Alfred Verling. From what he'd heard, he didn't think Douglas was that kind of man.

He dipped down into a deep gully, followed the bottom for a mile or more, then climbed out of the ravine in a series of switchbacks. When he reached the top, Douglas was not more than fifty yards from him. He stopped, waiting until the sheriff rode up, then raised a hand in greeting.

'Howdy, Buck,' Dan said.

The sheriff nodded, his bronze face showing no expression. He said, 'Hot day, ain't it, Dan?'

'Hot for this time of year,' Dan agreed, and wiped his face with his bandanna.

There was a moment of uneasy silence, the sheriff's gray eyes probing Dan's as if curious about this meeting. Dan had rehearsed what he wanted to say a dozen times, but now that the actual moment of meeting was here, he realized that the direct approach which he had intended to make was wrong.

'Headed for Craig?' Douglas asked casually.

'No, I figured you'd be coming today and I wanted to talk to you before you got to the Hole.' Dan swung his horse around, adding, 'No use sitting here in the hot sun. Charley Klein might have a drink waiting for us. You can bunk with me tonight if you ain't particular about the company you keep.'

Douglas laughed. He was about fifty, a tall, hard-muscled man who had made his own way since he'd been a small boy. Dan knew that the sheriff's ranch had given him a living and he probably would have preferred to have kept on ranching, but the last sheriff had died in office and his deputy who ran at the next election was not considered capable of handling the

45

job, so several of Douglas's neighbors had urged him to run.

He had visited Smith's Hole just before the election trying to drum up votes. He had been so successful that there had not been a single vote cast against him, a fact that Dan hoped he remembered.

'I ain't so particular as all that,' Douglas said as he swung in beside Dan. 'I ain't ever sampled your cooking, but I'll risk it.'

'Laura Bailey's a neighbor of mine,' Dan said. 'Maybe we can get supper at her place. She's a damned good cook.' He paused and added, 'I don't figure she's got any fresh beef, though. Pork maybe, or a chicken, but no beef.'

Douglas was startled and showed it. He glanced at Dan, who stared straight ahead. Presently the sheriff said, 'Now it's downright interesting that you mention Mrs. Bailey. It's likewise interesting that you mentioned fresh beef. I guess the most interesting part of all is the fact that you rode out here to meet me.'

'Well, it wasn't no accident,' Dan admitted. 'We figure that you were tipped off that Laura had butchered a Skull steer and you'd find the hide hid somewhere around her place. I can tell you where to look. It's rolled up under a manger in her barn, but you can hunt till you're black in the face and you won't find no evidence of any butchering around her place.'

Douglas stroked his chin, his gaze still on Dan's face. 'Just what are you trying to tell me,

Matson? I ain't sure I'm reading between the lines what I'm supposed to read.'

'All right, I'll make it plain,' Dan said, 'though I figure you're reading it right. I was on my way to a meeting in Charley Klein's saloon this morning when Laura yelled at me to stop. She took me into the barn and showed me a Skull hide that was shoved under a manger and told me that during the night their dog got excited and Bess got up to see what was going on. She didn't find nothing, but they got to looking this morning and found the hide. It seems that somebody had rode in, hid the hide, and got out before Bess could dress and leave the house. This somebody must have been a Skull man trying to frame Laura and Bess for rustling to get them out of the Hole.'

'Well now, that is an interesting theory,' Douglas murmured.

'No theory,' Dan said sharply. 'Buck, you know what's going on out here. You answer me one question. Who tipped you off about the hide?'

'You'd never guess,' Douglas said softly, smiling as he said it. 'Judge Verling.'

'How did he hear about it?'

'He wouldn't tell me, which same made me a little suspicious,' Douglas said. 'He claimed he had some informants among the lawless men in this part of the country and he couldn't risk giving out any names, even to me. I guess it's true that you've got a couple of men living out here who are wanted by the law.'

'Texas law,' Dan said quickly. 'I don't figure you're interested in enforcing Texas law.'

'No, I sure ain't,' Douglas said, 'not as long as these men keep their noses clean in my ballywick. I decided I'd better take a *pasear* out here, but I want you to pass the word along that I ain't figuring on shipping anybody back to Texas. It might save trouble later on if these boys know that.'

'Now maybe Judge Verling might be more interested than you are in enforcing Texas law,' Dan said.

Douglas nodded. 'You're right about that. In fact, he's been after me to arrest these two men, but I keep telling him I don't know nothing about it. He gets so damned mad.' Douglas laughed. 'I guess me and the old judge just don't see things eye to eye.'

'Like Justin Albright moving his herd into the Hole,' Dan said.

Douglas nodded. 'And any shenanigans Albright might have his hand in.' He paused, then went on, 'What I really rode out here for was to talk to you and some of the others about what's ahead for all of us. I don't want to have to arrest any of you for murder. I know, and so do you, that if it comes to showdown with Albright, there'll be some killings.'

He pointed the forefinger of his right hand at Dan pistol-like. 'If that happens, I'll be in one hell of a squeeze. No matter how my sympathies lie, most of the Hole is public domain and Albright's got as much right to run his cattle on it as you have. On the other hand, I know how you people feel. I'd feel the same if I lived here, but damn it, the law is the law. There's only about so much looking the other way that I can do.'

This was exactly what Dan had expected to hear and it was the last thing he wanted to hear. He was silent for a time, the upper walls of Maroon canyon closing in on them. Finally he asked, 'What did you think when Verling told you about the hide?'

'I figured it was a plant,' Douglas said, 'but I decided to pretend to look into it to satisfy the judge, seeing as I don't pay much attention to most of the things he says. Hell, if I tried looking into every beef that was butchered by someone just for eating, I'd run my horse's legs off.'

He shook his head. 'Actually it didn't make much sense, thinking that a Skull steer would wander into the Hole for Mrs. Bailey to butcher, or that she and Bess would ride out to the Little Snake and butcher a Skull steer. No, I had no intention of arresting either one of the Bailey women. I dunno what's back of it, though. Maybe it's just a smoke screen to get our eyes off the main trick.'

'I hadn't thought of that,' Dan said. 'We've got Lee Jackson locked up in Charley's saloon.

49

We figured you'd want to talk to him.'

'Locked up? Why?'

Dan told him what had happened, adding, 'It was personal between me 'n' Jackson, but as long as he was there, we thought we'd keep him till you got here. He wouldn't tell us nothing about that hide, but he might talk to you.'

'Maybe,' Douglas said, 'but did you think that he may charge you and your friends with kidnapping?'

'No, I didn't,' Dan admitted, 'but you'd have a hell of a time making an arrest on that charge.'

'Yeah, maybe I would,' Douglas said.

His tone was plain, Dan thought. He might as well have said not to push him and that was something Dan had no intention of doing.

CHAPTER SEVEN

Lee Jackson had lost all sense of time. He knew only one thing. He had to get out of this prison of a room or he'd go crazy. He still hurt from Matson's punishing blows, but he wasn't dizzy now. He could ride if he could get free.

He pounded on the door; he tried to smash it open but it wouldn't give. All he gained was a bruised shoulder. He glanced at the tiny window as he had a dozen times and shook his head. There was no escape that way.

He sat down on the bed and held his head and cursed. Later, much later it seemed, the door opened and Bess Bailey came in. She asked, 'You feel like riding?'

He got to his feet. 'You're damned right I do. Just give me my gun and I'll slope out of here. If I ever see this hole in the ground again, it will be too soon.'

'You ain't riding for a minute or two,' Bess said. 'The sheriff wants to talk to you.'

Jackson had reached the door. Now he wheeled around to face Bess. 'What kind of a game is this? I ain't done nothing that would concern the sheriff.'

'Tell him that yourself, Jackson,' Bess said.

'I will,' Jackson said. 'I sure as hell will.'

He turned back and lunged through the doorway, his fists clenched, anger boiling up in him. He supposed the Hole men were still here and he wondered what kind of punishment they had stored up for him this time, but when he looked around the saloon, he saw that most of the men were gone. Only old Charley Klein was slouched near the door, Dan Matson sat at one of the tables, and the sheriff stood with his back to the bar.

'Howdy, Lee,' the lawman said amiably. 'Matson tells me they held you here so I could talk to you. This wasn't any of my doing, you understand. Do you want to bring charges against them for assault and battery?

Kidnapping? Restraining you by force against your will?'

'No, by God,' Jackson fumed. 'I've had more 'n enough of all of 'em. I just want out of here. I'll tell you something else. I ain't broke no laws, so there's nothing you've got to talk to me about.' He turned to face Bess. 'Give me my gun.'

'Now hold on,' Douglas said. 'I aim to ask you a few questions, but I'm not accusing you of anything. I'm glad you don't want to press charges against these people because I don't think it would hold up in court. They had no legal right to hold you, but I savvy why they feel the way they do after the way your boss has been threatening them.'

Jackson wished he hadn't decided so quickly not to press charges. Maybe it wouldn't be as hard to make it stick as Douglas had said with Judge Verling holding court, then knew at once that the sheriff was right for the simple reason that when it came down to cases, Douglas wouldn't arrest any of them.

Jackson had heard Justin Albright and the judge talk about Douglas. They hated and feared him. He might not be on the side of the Hole ranchers, but he certainly wasn't on Albright's side, either.

For a moment Jackson hesitated, his gaze turning briefly to Matson who was staying out of the conversation. He didn't savvy this. Apparently he wasn't going to have any more trouble with Matson, but trouble with Buck Douglas might be worse.

'All right,' he said finally. 'You fixing to arrest me because I'm working for Justin Albright?'

'No,' Douglas said. 'I'm not fixing to arrest you at all. Not today anyhow. I want you to tell me about the hide that Laura Bailey found.'

'Hide?' Jackson had forgotten all about it. 'By God, I don't know nothing about no hide. I told 'em that. Framing a woman for rustling ain't my style and you know it.'

'But it's Justin Albright's style,' Douglas said. 'It don't make no sense for Laura and Bess Bailey to butcher a Skull steer. Now I'm going to the Bailey place from here. If I find they ain't lying and I see that hide like Matson and Bess have told me, then I'm going to think that Albright is running a sandy on all of us.'

'It ain't none of my doing,' Jackson said sourly.

'I've known Albright a long time,' the sheriff said. 'Longer 'n you have, Jackson. I know that among other things he's a thief and a liar. A man like that with the power and money he's got can raise hell and prop it up with a chunk.'

'I tell you it ain't none of my doing,' Jackson said doggedly. 'I work for him and I do what he tells me. If he's running a sandy, it ain't none of my responsibility.'

'No, Lee, you're going to be responsible,' Douglas said mildly. 'You'd better start getting used to the idea. Now, the law is on his side as far as using the public domain is concerned. You know as well as I do that the people who live here will fight and there'll be some killings. That's where I come in. You, too. You bring your crew in here and I'll hold you responsible for what happens. These people will die for their homes. We both know that.'

'Oh no, you won't hold me responsible,' Jackson snarled. 'Not if they attack us and kill some of my men.'

'I will,' Douglas said. 'I know how these people feel. I'd do the same if I was in their boots. It's your choice. You can quit working for a man like Albright, or you can go on and maybe put a rope around your neck.'

'Just give me my gun,' Jackson bellowed at Bess. 'I keep telling you that all I want is to get out of here.'

Douglas glanced at Matson, who gave a bare half-inch nod, and he in turn nodded at Bess. She turned to a shelf behind her and took down the belt and gun. She said, 'You'll get a warmer welcome the next time you come to Smith's Hole.'

He jerked the belt out of her hands. He buckled it around him as he strode toward the door, not looking back or saying a word. Just as he stepped out into the afternoon sunlight, Charley Klein said, 'I moved your horse around to the shed in back to get him out of the sun.'

54

Jackson went on, still not saying a word. As he rounded the corner of the building, Klein called, 'Just a minute, Jackson. I clean forgot about it, but I've got a letter for you. Been here two, three days. I guess somebody expected you to get here before you did.'

Jackson didn't break stride. He reached his horse, tightened the cinch, and untied him. He mounted and rode around the building. Klein stood in the road holding up a letter. Jackson jerked it out of his fingers, jammed it into his shirt pocket, and went on, spurring his horse into a run. He didn't even slow down as he passed Margo Lane's cabin.

When he reached Maroon canyon he reined down to a walk. He took a long, sighing breath, wondering how a man could survive a prison sentence. He had never lost his freedom before and he didn't want to lose it now.

The trail along the creek was in shadow and the air was cooler here, but Jackson didn't notice. All he could think of was Douglas's warning. If there was a fight, and there sure as hell was going to be the way things were shaping up, he'd be held responsible and he'd really lose his freedom.

A prickle ran down his spine as he thought about it. There would be no justice to it, he told himself over and over, but it was the way Douglas had said. He had a choice if he took it now. He could quit his job and tell Albright to go to hell. The old man was a robber. There was no doubt about that, but he was a big one, not a piker like Laura and Bess Bailey if they really had butchered a Skull steer.

Well, he'd thought about quitting Albright more than once. He remembered when he'd been a prisoner in Charley Klein's bedroom that he had decided he wasn't having any part of killing. He'd done enough of Albright's dirty work and the old bastard couldn't pay him enough for him to keep on doing it.

Then, as it always had been when he reached this stage of rebellion, he began having second thoughts. Albright paid him well. He would never find another job that paid as much as this one. He went back over his conversation with Margo; he thought about the little spread in North Park that he wanted to buy, and he went through the same mental arithmetic he always did when he reached this point in his thinking. The price of the ranch. The amount of money he had in the bank in Laramie. The amount he could save if he worked for Albright all winter.

He rode out of the steep-walled canyon, the late afternoon sunlight laying its bright sheen on the slanted red slopes. He took a long, sighing breath. Damn that Buck Douglas! He'd just put out a lot of scare talk.

How could any sheriff call it murder if a man was killed in a fight over grass? No jury would find him guilty in a case like this. He would be no more responsible than Matson or

Charley Klein or any of the other Hole men if it came to a finish fight and men were killed.

Suddenly the fury and fear and frustration of the day left him and he let himself dream of marrying Margo, of sleeping with her, of fathering her babies. He could ask for nothing more. To hell with Buck Douglas.

It would not be Lee Jackson's responsibility if some of the Hole men were killed trying to hold grass that did not belong to them. Skull would simply be claiming public domain that belonged to Justin Albright as much as to anyone. No sheriff, and that included Buck Douglas, could make it his responsibility.

Lee Jackson found himself at peace. He had argued himself into that state of mind many times in the last six months. He had done it again.

CHAPTER EIGHT

Dan Matson and Buck Douglas stood on the porch of Charley Klein's saloon watching Lee Jackson ride away. Klein, who had been standing in front, now turned and trudged past Dan and the sheriff, muttering, 'Damned ungrateful pup. I'm gonna get out of this heat. You boys come in and I'll give you a beer.'

Neither man moved until Jackson was in Maroon canyon and out of sight. Douglas said finally, 'Well, what do you make of him, Dan?'

'I figured from the first that he had nothing to do with the hides,' Dan answered. 'That means somebody else is working around him doing what Albright wants done. If I was Jackson, I wouldn't stand still for that.'

'Jackson ain't you,' Douglas said. 'I think you're right. There's a fellow named Orly Hunt in Jackson's crew who used to ramrod that outfit. Know him?'

Dan nodded. 'He's been here a few times, getting mail, but he's an old codger.'

'Not too old to butcher a Skull steer unbeknownst to Jackson and ride over here and hide it in the Bailey barn,' Douglas said. 'Years ago when I knew him he was a little more spry than he is now. They wintered on White river in those days. Hunt retired and was living in Laramie the last I heard, but damned if he didn't show up in Craig a month or so ago and said he was riding for Jackson. That didn't look right to me then and it still don't.'

'You figure he got his orders straight from Albright?'

'That's exactly what I figure,' Douglas said. 'Now I don't peg Jackson as being very sharp, but I think he's straight, straight enough that he wouldn't try to frame a woman and her girl. How far he'll go carrying out Albright's orders when it comes to moving into the Hole is something I don't know.'

'You gave him a few mouthfuls to chew on,' Dan said. 'Well, you ready to ride?'

'I'm ready.'

Dan turned back into the saloon. 'We'll take that free beer some other time, Charley,' he said. 'We're riding, Bess.'

'I'll tag along,' she said. 'Keep your eyes peeled, Charley.'

'I'll do that,' the old man said. 'You and Laura do the same.'

'Charley, tell everybody you see that next Saturday we'll get together at Lone Rock and pile up some dry wood,' Dan said. 'Have 'em bring axes. Tell 'em to be there by nine o'clock, and tell 'em to pass the word.'

'We'll have a feed at the schoolhouse that evening,' Bess added. 'Have 'em tell their wives to fix some beans and potato salad and pies and such.'

'I'll tell 'em,' Klein said, grinning. 'I'll even fetch one of my pies, seeing as I'm not much good with an ax no more.'

'Never mind,' Bess said. 'I'll have Ma bake an extra pie so all you'll have to do is eat.'

Klein snickered. 'Afraid to eat one of my pies, ain't you?'

'We've got cause to be afraid,' Dan said. 'Remember that pup I fed a piece of your pie to the last time you baked one? Hell, he fell over and died before he could say thank you.'

Dan followed Douglas around the saloon to the shed where their horses were tied. A

59

moment later Bess joined them, saying, 'Old Charley's a good bartender, but he's one hell of a poor cook.'

'I was glad to hear you talk about the feed,' Dan said. 'It's a good thing for us to eat together, considering what's ahead for us. I reckon you'll be helping your ma bake those pies.'

'I won't do no such thing,' Bess snapped. 'I'll fetch an ax and be up there on top of Lone Rock with the rest of you.'

Dan had expected her to say that. Well, she'd have to do it, he thought sourly as he tightened the cinch and swung into leather. He glanced at Bess wondering how she'd look in a dress. It had been a long time since he'd seen her wear anything but men's clothes. She'd be a damned fine-looking woman if she'd let herself.

He headed upstream, Douglas reining in beside him. A moment later Bess joined them. She said, 'Sheriff, you're not going to let that Skull herd come into the Hole, are you?'

He gave her a questioning look, then he said slowly, 'My job is to enforce the law. I don't make it. The law says Albright has got the right to use this grass as well as anybody as long as it's open range.'

'Damn it, Douglas,' Bess exploded, 'that's a pussyfooting answer and you know it. You got any idea what's going to happen if they drive that herd in here?'

'I've got a very good idea,' Douglas answered, troubled.

'Well, do something,' she snapped.

'Miss Bailey, will you tell me what I can do?'

She hesitated, glancing at Dan who was scowling at her, then turned back to Douglas. 'No, I can't tell you, but you don't expect us to just walk out of the Hole and leave our homes we've had for years, the home where I was born and where my pa's buried?'

'I wish you would,' Douglas said, 'but I don't figure you will.'

'Well then, do something to stop it,' Bess fumed.

'I can't do anything about a crime until it's committed,' Douglas said. 'I'll wait and hope that Albright is bluffing or will make a mistake. If he breaks a law, I'll get him. The trouble is Jackson is the one I'll have to take and he ain't to blame.'

'You can't count on a man like Albright making a mistake,' Dan said.

'I ain't so sure,' Douglas said thoughtfully. 'A big man keeps wanting to get bigger, and after while he gets loco enough to think he's so big he can bend the law to suit himself. I think Albright is that kind of man.'

After that they rode in uneasy silence, Bess making no effort to hide her anger and Dan wishing she'd kept her mouth shut. When they reached the Bailey place, Mrs. Bailey ran out of the house, her long shadow racing beside

61

her across the dusty yard.

'Good evening, Mr. Douglas,' she said. 'We'll show you where the hide is. I guess you've heard about it by now.'

'Yes, I have,' he said.

'You going to arrest us?'

'I certainly am not,' he assured her. 'I'll look at the hide and ride back to town and tell Judge Verling no crime was committed. All I'm asking is that you don't say anything about it. Of course, it will get out, but the less said, the better.'

'Meanwhile maybe we can mooch a meal off of you, Laura,' Dan said. 'The sheriff is bunking with me tonight.'

'Of course,' Mrs. Bailey said. 'I don't have time to fix an old hen, so we'll have ham.'

She glanced at Bess as if hoping her daughter would come into the kitchen with her, but Bess dismounted, saying, 'I'll cut some wood as soon as I take care of my horse.'

'Oh, one thing, Mrs. Bailey,' Douglas said. 'I'd like to look around and see that there ain't a beef hanging anywhere on your property. I know I won't find one, but I want to answer Judge Verling's questions when he quizzes me which he's gonna do.'

'Look all you want to,' Laura Bailey called over her shoulder as she walked back across the yard to the kitchen.

Douglas and Dan watered their horses at the log trough beside the corral gate. Douglas said, 'She's been worrying, all right. Maybe I should have gone ahead and looked without saying anything to her.'

'Oh, you've got to do your duty, Sheriff,' Bess said as she stripped gear off her horse. 'A man's got to do what he's got to do, don't he, Dan?'

'That's right,' Dan said. 'So does a woman.'

Douglas followed Dan into the barn and waited while Dan pulled the hide out from under the manger. The sheriff unrolled it, glanced at the brand, and smiled faintly. 'A rustler would have cut out the brand, wouldn't he?'

'Or she,' Bess said from the doorway in her edgy voice. 'Even a woman rustler would be smart enough to do that. Now you go ahead and hunt, damn it.'

She wheeled away and strode toward the house. Douglas handed the hide back to Dan. He said, 'I guess they've got a right to be hot under the collar. If I was Albright's man, this would be excuse enough to arrest 'em and they know it. All right, let's start looking.'

They spent an hour searching the house and outbuildings, but failed to turn up any meat except the hams and bacon hanging from the ceiling of the smokehouse.

They returned to the kitchen, Douglas saying, 'Mrs. Bailey, we didn't find anything I knew we wouldn't, but I thought I ought to go through the motions. Now I can tell the judge that me and Matson had thoroughly gone over your buildings and found no incriminating evidence. I don't figure the hide was by itself.'

Laura Bailey was stirring gravy at the stove. She said, 'Sit down, both of you. I'll have supper on the table in a minute.' She took a long breath that was almost a sob, then she said, 'It's been a long day, Mr. Douglas.'

'It was a lowdown thing for Albright to do,' Douglas said. 'I ain't real sure why he done it unless he's got something else up his sleeve that's a lot worse and he done this just to make you folks jumpy.'

'He done that, all right,' Bess said.

After they finished eating, Dan said, 'Don't forget to bake them pies for Saturday. I guess Bess told you what we're fixing to do.'

'She told me,' Mrs. Bailey said. 'Thank you, Mr. Douglas.'

He nodded. 'Thank you for supper,' he said, and followed Dan out of the house and across the yard to the corral.

Neither talked as they rode on to Dan's place. It was dark when they reined up in front of the corral, the light from a full moon working through the clouds. Douglas said, 'I dunno why I ever ran for the sheriff's job. I used to think that wrong was wrong and right was right, but it didn't take me long to see that it ain't so. Trouble is the law's not much help in a case like this. It might be different if old man Verling wasn't . . .'

'Take it real easy,' a man said from the shadows beside the barn. 'No fast moves. Now hook the moon, lawman. You, too, Dan.'

CHAPTER NINE

Lee Jackson reached the cow camp at dusk. He hunkered by the fire, a cup of coffee in his hands as Orly Hunt parted the willows on the south bank of the Little Snake and walked toward him, a fishing pole in his hands.

'Catch anything?' Jackson asked.

'No.' Hunt squatted beside Jackson. 'You said you'd be back by the middle of the afternoon.'

Jackson stared at his nearly empty cup, fighting to hold his temper in check. It would do no good to quarrel with Orly Hunt. He was one of Justin Albright's favorites. The man had retired several years ago, and why he had showed up this summer to ride with the Skull crew was more than Jackson could understand.

Hunt was not an old man, but he was past his prime, the years in the saddle having taken their toll. Jackson had never worked under him, but he'd seen him around Laramie and knew him by sight. Albright had sent word that Hunt was to take over if for any reason Jackson was gone. But damn it, he wasn't gone, and still Hunt was making him account for his time when it wasn't any of Hunt's business.

'I got delayed,' Jackson said finally. 'They ganged up on me. I was lucky to get out of the Hole alive.'

'I figured you were loco to go down there,' Hunt said. 'Hear from the boss?'

'No.' Suddenly he remembered the letter Charley Klein had given him. He had jammed it into his pocket without a glance. 'Wait a minute. Maybe I did.'

He took the letter out of his pocket, tore it open, and, holding it close to the flames, read it. Then he sat staring at it, not knowing what to make of it.

'Well?' Hunt prodded.

'Yeah, I heard from him, all right,' Jackson said. 'I didn't get this letter until I was leaving and I forgot all about it. The boss wants me to come to Denver and meet him in his room in the Windsor Hotel Monday night. Hell, I don't think I can make it'

'You can if you ride all night,' Hunt said. 'You'll just about catch the morning stage to Steamboat Springs.'

'I'm tired,' Jackson said sullenly. 'I took a beating and I hurt.'

'You'll go,' Hunt said as if there was no question about it. 'I've worked off and on for the old bastard for twenty years. He don't change. I've sure learned one thing about him. You do what he says or you quit. There's no

66

room in between. Take planting that hide in the Bailey women's barn. I didn't like doing it, but that was his orders.'

'You done that?' Jackson demanded. 'They kept blaming me for it.'

'Chances are that's why he had me do it,' Hunt said. 'He's a smart old boy. He figures you'd go down there into the Hole, being sweet on the schoolteacher like you are, and they'd jump you. Well, if you didn't know nothing about it, you couldn't tell 'em nothing.'

For a time Jackson stared at Hunt in the dim light, resentment stirring in him. He'd have it out with Albright when he saw him, he told himself. Either he was going to run this end of things or Albright could find himself another man.

It wasn't just that framing a woman was dirty business, although it was and he would have balked at it. The part that hurt was the simple fact that Albright had gone around him without even informing him about the frame-up.

A moment later he knew he would make no threat to Albright about finding another man. He'd swallow his pride and keep his mouth shut. You simply didn't threaten Justin Albright. It was the way Hunt had just said it was. You did what Albright ordered or you quit. The hell of it was there were always men like Hunt who would do what they were told.

'Why did he want to frame the Bailey women?' Jackson asked after a long pause.

'Why does he want you in Denver?' Hunt answered with a question of his own.

'He says he's got a plan that will end the resistance in the Hole,' Jackson said. 'He wants me to be there to help work it out. He also says that Judge Verling will be on hand, but I'm not to talk to him if I run into him before I get to Denver or even act like I know him. I'm to come to Albright's room alone. I don't see . . .'

'No, you don't see,' Hunt said somberly, 'but for your own safety, I'd say you'd better have no connection with Verling. Later on you can say you didn't even see Albright when you were in Denver. If Buck Douglas asks you why you went, tell him you were there to go to the best whorehouse you could find because there ain't nothing good in Craig or Steamboat Springs. He'll savvy that. Maybe you'd better go, too, just to make your story stick in case Douglas starts checking it.'

Jackson shook his head. 'I don't know what you're driving at.'

Hunt shrugged. 'I ain't sure myself, but the old son of a bitch is up to something. I don't know what it is, but I figure it's bad. That's why he had me plant that hide. I don't think he figured that Douglas would arrest the Bailey women, but it's bound to make 'em uneasy, maybe scare 'em. It might not take much more

68

to make 'em panic and pull out of the Hole. It's an old trick. I've used it plenty of times. You hit a man on one side and when he looks in that direction, you move in and knock him out from the other side.'

'Well, they're uneasy, all right,' Jackson said bitterly. 'Scared, too, maybe. That was why they held me.'

'Funny thing about old Justin,' Hunt said thoughtfully. 'You're purty new with him, but I've known him for years. That's why he sent for me to ride with your crew for a couple of months. He knows I'll do whatever he tells me no matter what it is.'

He picked up a stick and threw it into the fire. 'You see, if I don't get killed doing his dirty work for him, I've got my old age taken care of. He's pensioned me, providing I do what he says once in a while if he needs me. I don't want your job, Lee. That ain't why I'm here.'

He nodded, saying, 'I wondered about it.'

'Now I'm wondering about something,' Hunt said. 'How far will you go with his scheming?'

Jackson rose and dropped his coffee cup into the wreck pan. 'I don't know,' he said. 'I guess it depends on what his scheme is. I keep telling myself I'm my own man and I'll do what I think I ought to do, but damn it, I always wind up following his orders. I need the job till spring, then I figure to get married and buy my

69

own outfit, so I guess I'll hang on until then.'

'You'll hang on.' Hunt was amused. 'Will you hang on until you hang? For murder?'

Jackson was startled. He had thought vaguely about this, but he had not believed Albright would go that far. Well, it was plain that Hunt thought he would.

Still, it seemed to him that Albright had too much to lose to risk it. The grass in Smith's Hole wasn't worth it. He shook his head. 'He's too smart for that.'

Hunt smiled. He asked softly, 'How smart is smart?' Jackson didn't answer, so Hunt went on, 'It's been my experience that a smart man winds up at a place where he can't back up. I never murdered anybody for him, but he's bigger and smarter than when I used to run this outfit. I'm thinking that maybe I'm paying too big a price for my pension. Maybe you'll pay too big a price keeping your job till spring.'

He picked up his fishing pole and rose. 'I've got too much invested to pull out now, but you're young with a lot of living ahead of you I don't have.' He turned away, adding, 'I'll do what he says if it kills me.'

Jackson thought about it all the way to Craig. For the first time he felt he knew Orly Hunt. Certainly he had talked more to him tonight than he had since he'd showed up with his note from Albright a month ago.

It hadn't added up right, Hunt's coming back to ride after being retired for several

70

years. Now it looked worse, that Albright was willing to sacrifice Lee Jackson and he wanted a man with the herd he could depend on who would take over.

Thinking back over his conversation with Hunt, it seemed that the man was advising him to get out while he could. Well, he'd see what Albright had to say in Denver. There was still time.

CHAPTER TEN

Dan Matson and Buck Douglas froze when they heard the order to hook the moon. Dan instantly recognized the voice as Lige Carter's, but it was not his normal friendly voice. For a moment he didn't know what to do. He sensed that Carter was wound up until he was close to a killing mood.

'Hoist 'em, Buck,' Dan said softly. 'We don't want to set him off.'

'That's better,' Carter said when the hands of both men were raised. 'A whole lot better. Now Mr. Star Toter, I've got something to say to you. If you think you're sending us back to Texas . . .'

'Hold on, Lige,' Dan interrupted. 'Let's go into the house. I'll put the coffee pot on the stove. If I stand here like this, I'm gonna get mighty damned tired keeping my hands up.'

71

'And give Douglas a chance to go for his gun?' Carter asked. 'No, we'll stay right here with you gents in the moonlight so we can see any move you make. Maybe I'd better warn you that Nate is standing behind you. If you get foxy, he'll blow your lamp out.'

'I have no intention of sending you back to Texas,' Douglas said. 'I likewise have no intention of getting foxy, so just let us go about our business.'

'Like getting the drop on us and throwing us into the jug so you can collect the reward.' Carter spat the words at him. 'All of you God-damned star toters are the same.'

'I knew you were here,' Douglas said. 'If I'd wanted that reward, I'd have been out here a long time ago.'

'Why weren't you?' Carter demanded.

'I figured it would be the hardest money I ever earned,' Douglas said. 'It wasn't worth it.'

Carter laughed, a high-pitched sound as unnatural as his voice. He was scared and worried, Dan sensed, and that made him as dangerous as a cornered mountain lion.

'You were sure dead right about that,' Carter said. 'Now suppose you tell us what your business is if you wasn't after us.'

'I had a tip that Mrs. Bailey had stolen a Skull steer and butchered it,' Douglas said.

'That's just about as loco as coming after me 'n' Nate,' Carter said. 'Well, you ain't taking Mrs. Bailey to the calaboose. You ain't taking nobody out of the Hole.'

'I ain't fixing to,' Douglas snapped angrily. 'I keep telling you . . .'

'Me 'n' Nate rode a long ways to find this place,' Carter went on as if he didn't hear Douglas talking. 'Now we've lived peaceable for quite a while. We don't aim to see things busted up around here. You come nosing around our end of the Hole and you'll get a window in your skull.'

'My God, can't you listen to me just once?' Douglas said. 'I ain't here to bust nothing up. Me 'n' Matson decided Mrs. Bailey didn't steal no steer.'

'That's right, Lige,' Dan said.

For a moment Lige Carter was silent, apparently thinking about what Douglas had said. Finally he asked, 'What are you gonna do about the Skull herd coming into the Hole?'

'Nothing,' Douglas said. 'Albright ain't breaking a law by using this grass. If anybody stops him, you people in the Hole will have to do it.'

'And then you'll come in here with a posse to arrest us for killing some of Albright's men,' Carter said bitterly. 'That's the God-damned law for you. It made an outlaw out of me years ago and kept me running ever since. You can talk about law and justice till you get calluses on your tongue, but they ain't the same thing. Not by a hell of a lot.'

'Lige, you'd better think about one thing,'

73

Dan said. 'Buck Douglas is on our side more 'n the next sheriff would be if Albright has anything to do with the election. Verling has been on Douglas's tail to come in after you and Nate. Well, if we get another sheriff, he'll probably do what Verling says. Remember Verling says and does what Albright wants him to.'

From somewhere in the shadows behind Dan and Douglas, Nate Willets said, 'That sounds reasonable, Lige. Let's let 'em go as long as the sheriff don't come poking around the upper end of the Hole.'

'Just one thing before you ride off,' Douglas said. 'I don't care how much Texas wants you. If anybody takes you back to Texas, it'll be a U.S. Marshal or a Texas lawman. Just don't break no Colorado laws or I will come back and take you in.'

Carter laughed. 'You ain't in no shape to take nobody in, Sheriff. I've got a good notion to smoke you down right where you stand. If some other lawman comes smelling around here, he'll get a dose of hot lead, too.'

'No, Lige,' Willets said. 'I've done just as much running as you have, but Dan's right about us being better off with Douglas wearing the star than some jasper Albright helps pick.'

'Sure I'm right, Lige,' Dan said. 'We'd better save our fighting for Albright and his crew when they show up in the Hole.'

Silence then that ribboned out into what

seemed an eternity. For Dan, standing there in the moonlight with his hands over his head, the pressure was too much to stand. He could feel Carter's hatred and fear bearing down on the lawman, a hatred that had gone back years into Carter's life and now was a virulent poison in him. If he gave way to it and killed Douglas, he'd have to kill Dan, too.

For this seemingly endless moment of time the tension seemed unbearable. Sweat poured down Dan's face; his belly flattened against his backbone, so cold that it was paralyzed. Then Carter said unexpectedly, 'Let's ride.'

A few seconds later the sound of hoofbeats came to Dan. He took a long breath as he put his hands down, saying, 'That was close. I thought I knew Lige Carter, but I never seen him that way before. He was in the store this morning with Willets. They wanted to cut Jackson up. They acted like they was joshing, but I don't think they were. I guess they rode home, thought about it, and decided to bear down on you.'

'They done it for a fact,' Douglas said. 'I knew it was close. Any time you have a man like Carter pointing a gun at you with his finger on the trigger, it's close.'

They took care of their horses and walked across the yard to the house, Dan saying, 'I'll build a fire if you want a cup of coffee before we go to bed.'

'Not tonight,' Douglas said. 'It's too hot to

build a fire.'

Dan led the way into the house, struck a match, and lighted a lamp. He motioned with a sweeping gesture toward the unmade bed, the dirty dishes stacked on a work table near the range, and the clutter of bridles, saddles, leather straps, almanacs, and newspapers in one corner of the room.

'A boar's nest,' Dan said apologetically.

'You need a woman,' Douglas said, smiling. 'If you ever come to see me, you can say the same thing.'

Dan pulled a chair back from the table. He said, 'Sit down if you ain't sleepy.'

'Not yet.' Douglas took the chair, removed his hat, and laid it on the table. 'You know, I don't blame Carter for feeling the way he does. If they're the men I think they are, and I'm sure they are from what I've heard, Carter took a hell of a beating because some flibberty gibbet of a girl claimed he'd looked at her too long or some damned thing.

'It seems that Willets worked on the same spread. I guess him and Carter were good friends. Anyhow, they waited till they had a chance at the leader of the gang that done the beating and they damned near killed him. He was the local bully. You know the kind, tough as all hell when he's got his bunch with him, but a coward by himself.

'Of course, the sheriff took after Carter and Willets, but he hadn't turned a hand after

Carter got his beating. The thing wound up with Carter killing the sheriff when he tried to arrest both of 'em, and then of course they had to run. I can see why they got jumpy about having me in the Hole. Chances are this is the first time for years they can sleep without worrying about somebody turning them in for the reward money.'

'Lige didn't have to get as proddy as he did,' Dan said, 'but you're right about 'em being able to sleep. Nobody in the Hole is gonna turn 'em in for the reward money. Folks like 'em. We all know we need 'em if and when there's a fight. I was thinking this morning when we was in Charley's store that they're about the only two men I can count on if it comes to a showdown.'

'That's the part that worries me,' Douglas admitted. 'I don't want to take 'em in for a killing, or you, either, and I know damned well there's going to be a killing or maybe a dozen. Get something like this started and it turns into a last man feud.'

'There won't be any killing if the herd don't come in,' Dan said.

Douglas didn't say anything to that, but Dan knew what the sheriff was thinking, about the flow of events that was bound to come. It was as if Dan knew his destiny, as if he were reading a story, and by the time he was halfway through he knew what the end would be.

That night Dan slept very little. He lay

listening to the regular rhythm of Douglas's breathing, the prospect of becoming an outlaw a heavy weight on his mind. He could see only one ending to this story; he could feel the hangman's noose tightening around his neck.

The law was on Justin Albright's side, and in the end that was enough to pit Buck Douglas and his posse against the Hole men. This knowledge, he thought gloomily, was what had driven Lige Carter close to killing Buck Douglas.

CHAPTER ELEVEN

Lee Jackson rode hard all night and into the following morning, arriving in Craig an hour before the stage left. He turned his horse over to a hostler in a livery stable, ate breakfast, and stepped into the stage, noting that Judge Verling was not on board.

For a time Jackson was relieved. He wasn't sure that Verling had received the same instructions he had and the situation might be difficult if the judge wanted to be friendly. Jackson left the stage and got on the train at Steamboat Springs which was temporarily the end of steel. Just as the train started to leave, Verling ran from the nearest saloon and caught the last car.

Within a few minutes Jackson saw that he

had nothing to worry about. Verling took a seat in the opposite end of the smoker from Jackson, completely ignoring him. The judge laid his wide-brimmed white hat on the rack beside his valise, lighted up a stogy, and leaned back against the seat.

Verling reminded Jackson of Buffalo Bill Cody with his long white hair, his flowing white mustache and beard, and, Jackson thought sourly, he was as much of a fraud as Cody was. Jackson knew that the old man was liked and respected around Craig and Steamboat Springs, so apparently the average citizen never guessed how much he was under Justin Albright's orders.

But then maybe it didn't make any difference. No one in Moffat county was threatened by Albright except the people who lived in Smith's Hole, so, to most of the voters, the connection between Albright and Verling was no issue.

Jackson put his head back against the red plush seat, stretched his long legs in front of him, and dozed most of the way to Denver. The train pulled in late Monday afternoon. He took a room in a small hotel on Eighteenth Street, two blocks from the Windsor, had supper, and left the dining room at twenty minutes after seven. It would take him just about ten minutes to walk to the Windsor and find Albright's room. He had learned long ago that punctuality was a must for anyone

79

working for Justin Albright.

As he approached the Windsor, Jackson glanced up at the top of the five-story building. An American flag flew from the tallest tower, with the hotel's and British flags flying from the two smaller towers.

He shook his head as he thought about the values Justin Albright lived by. The Windsor was the natural place for the cowman to stay when he came to Denver. Money, power, prestige: these words seemed to fit the Windsor Hotel just as they fitted Albright.

Jackson strode through the main entrance on Larimer Street, on past the tall diamond dust minor in the hall, and, high heels cracking on the marble tiling, went on into the lobby, past the great walnut desk where countless famous and near-famous people had registered, and stepped into an elevator.

He rode to the fifth floor where the ceilings were not as high as on the lower floors, but where there was a magnificent view of the Rocky Mountains from the windows on the Eighteenth Street side. It would, Jackson reflected, be the proper floor for Albright.

He followed the hall to the room number Albright's letter had given him, the sound of his bootheels muffled by the heavy Brussels carpet. He knocked on the door, which was immediately opened by Judge Verling.

'Right on time, Lee,' Verling said genially, holding out his hand. 'Sorry I couldn't be sociable on the train.'

'Neither could I,' Jackson said, shaking Verling's hand.

'Come in,' Verling said. 'Mr. Albright is expecting you.'

Albright was standing by a window on the far side of the room, his eyes on the lighted street below him. Now he turned, calling, 'Yes, come in, Lee. I thought you'd be here on time. We need to talk a few minutes before Kurt Sparks arrives.'

Jackson stopped, flat-footed, his breath going out of him as violently as if he had been slugged in the belly. Everything that Hunt had hinted at was true. Cold-blooded murder was Justin Albright's plan. Kurt Sparks was the most notorious killer in the cattle country.

Albright made no effort to shake hands. Neither did Jackson. They stood staring at each other for several seconds, Albright smiling as if he enjoyed shocking his foreman, and Jackson laboring for breath as he told himself this was a nightmare; it could not really be happening.

Presently Albright nodded. 'I judge you are familiar with Sparks' record.' He motioned to a chair. 'Sit down, Lee. Here, have a cigar.'

He picked up a box from the bureau, flipped back the lid, and held it out to Jackson, who took one and sat down in the nearest chair. Albright gave Verling a cigar, took one himself, and set the box back on the bureau.

He took a full minute to bite off the end of the cigar, light it, and start puffing at it until he had it going. He made a ceremony out of it, being a man who never did a simple thing the simple way.

Jackson shoved the cigar into his coat pocket and continued to stare at Albright. The man was small, five feet five or six, and not heavily built, and yet he had a way of making others feel he was a very large and powerful man, and certainly an important one.

Jackson had never figured out how Albright achieved this. It might have been the way he held his shoulders, the dignity that he wrapped around himself like a coat, or maybe it was his deep voice that had the ring of power in it.

He was sixty or close to it, but he looked twenty years younger with no trace of gray in his hair or closely cropped mustache. He could, Jackson was sure, still fork a horse and turn in a good day's work on the range if he wanted to.

Albright had learned the cattle business the hard way, coming up the trail to Dodge City as a boy from Texas years ago. He saved his money, bought a small spread on the Laramie plains, and, with the help of a running iron, or so his enemies said, built up his herd until he had the biggest outfit in southern Wyoming. Later he had spread out into North Park in Colorado, and later into the northwestern part of the state and on into Utah.

In his younger years he had been handy with his gun. There was always an argument among people when they started talking about how many men he had killed. Some said a dozen, some less, and others more, but certainly there had been several.

Whether it was with a gun, or through the power of his bank in Laramie, or his control of public officials, Justin Albright had been an utterly ruthless man from the first. Jackson knew this very well, but it had never hit him as directly as it did now.

'I can't agree with you about hiring a man like Kurt Sparks,' Jackson said.

He was a little surprised at the sound of his voice. It came out clear and strong, and even as the words left his mouth, he was thinking that he had never talked to Justin Albright before in this manner.

Apparently Albright was not offended. He smiled a little. He had a way of being contemptuous of others who did not agree with him, and he clearly took that attitude now, assuming that Jackson actually did not have the temerity to criticize his action. He took the cigar out of his mouth and rolled it between his fingertips, his head bent forward, his sharp eyes pinned on Jackson's face.

'You're a good foreman, Lee,' Albright said tolerantly. 'You must know how important it is for us to have the grass in Smith's Hole.'

Jackson could have said it wasn't important

at all. This whole operation rested on the fact that Albright had decided to take the grass in Smith's Hole, that it was simply a whim, and he was going to bull it through regardless of the interest of the people who lived there.

But he didn't. Instead he said, 'We've wintered in other places before. We can do it this year. The herd is in excellent condition.'

'I'm glad to hear that,' Albright said, 'but the point is this. Those steers will be shipped early next summer. I want them to be in just as good condition then and not to come through the winter the way they usually do. If we winter in Smith's Hole, they'll be in good shape when we ship. I've seen that grass in other years, Lee. I doubt that it has changed much.'

Justin Albright was wearing a brown broadcloth suit, a white shirt, and a string tie, with a gold watch chain stretched across his chest, an elk tooth dangling from it. He was, in every way, a powerful and formidable man who was not to be argued with.

Still, Jackson continued to argue with him, telling himself that this was a time in his life when he could not afford to make a mistake, a moment that would likely decide his future. He said, 'Mr. Albright, hiring a man like Kurt Sparks means murder. He's a killer, and we'll all wind up hanging with him.'

'I think not,' Albright said. 'I don't like the word killer. Let's call him an exterminator. He is not known in Smith's Hole, so no one will recognize him. Furthermore, he will not under any circumstances involve us.'

Albright paused and pulled on his cigar, his eyes narrowing. 'Lee, you know and I know that the two men in Smith's Hole who will give us trouble are the worst kind of outlaws who should have been sent back to Texas to hang years ago. They would have been if we had an efficient sheriff in Moffat county. It will benefit everyone concerned to have these men taken care of.'

Jackson nodded, remembering being knocked down by Dan Matson in Charley Klein's saloon and hearing the voices of two men who wanted to eat his liver and send his heart to Albright. He was sure those two men were Lige Carter and Nate Willets, and he was also sure they would have done exactly what they said if Matson had not stopped them.

He had to agree with Albright. If those two men were killed, it would take the guts out of the Hole men, and there would be no resistance when the Skull herd was driven into the Hole.

'You don't need to worry about the law, Lee,' Verling said. 'I've never had a trial I couldn't handle. I can't control Buck Douglas, but I can and will control what goes on in my court.'

A heavy fist knocked on the door. Albright nodded at Verling. 'That will be Sparks. Let him in, Judge.'

Albright was smiling again, the same contemptuous smile that Jackson had seen a moment before. The cowman had known all the time that it would take very little to knock Jackson's objections down, and in that moment a shocking insight came to Lee Jackson. He knew now why Justin Albright had become a big man, and he knew equally well that he would be a small man as long as he lived.

CHAPTER TWELVE

Judge Verling opened the door, Kurt Sparks walked into the room, and Verling shut the door behind him. Jackson had heard about the gunman only in general terms. He had no idea what Sparks would be like, but now, his gaze pinned on the man, he told himself he should have guessed. Kurt Sparks looked exactly the way Jackson would have imagined a paid killer to look.

Sparks was big, an inch or so taller than Jackson with such wide shoulders that his body formed a rough triangle. He wore ordinary range clothes and carried a gun, but there was nothing extraordinary about that.

Still, no one would have mistaken the man for a run-of-the-mill cowhand. There was a cold arrogance about him that set him apart from the average rider, an arrogance so pronounced that Jackson felt he and Verling were shut out of any agreement that would be made here tonight, that Albright and Sparks were the only men of consequence here.

Sparks' nose was unusually long; his lips were so thin that his mouth gave the appearance of a long scar across the bottom of his face. He had black hair and eyes, and his skin was darker than the average white man, but whether this was caused by spending his waking hours out of doors or whether he had the blood of some other race in his ancestry was something Jackson could not decide.

Sparks made no effort to extend his hand. He gave Albright a small nod, completely ignoring both Verling and Jackson. A chill raveled down Jackson's back. It was as if a cold breath of air had come into the room. For the first time in his life, Lee Jackson had the experience of hating a man the instant he saw him.

Sparks stood just inside the door, silent and motionless, his gaze on Albright as if waiting for him to say something. He was utterly indifferent to anything or anyone else in the room but Justin Albright. It would take this kind of man, Jackson thought, to be an 'exterminator,' a man without normal human emotions.

'I asked you here because I want you to do a job for me in Smith's Hole,' Albright said after what seemed an eternity. 'Two men. Their names are Lige Carter and Nate Willets.'

Sparks gave another hint of a nod. 'They'll be taken care of. Five hundred dollars for each. I expect to be paid before I leave the county.'

'A man riding with my outfit on the Little Snake named Orly Hunt has the money,' Albright said. 'Contact him.' He motioned to Jackson. 'This is my foreman, Lee Jackson. Lee, tell him about these two men.'

'Carter is a Negro and a first class cowboy,' Jackson said. 'Nate Willets has been a gunhand, or so they say. Both are from Texas and are supposed to be running from the law. They have the only spreads in the north end of the Hole.'

Sparks acted as if he had not heard. He still looked at Albright, purposely giving the impression that he did not consider either Jackson or Verling worth noticing. He asked, 'Anyone else?'

Jackson said quickly, 'No.'

Albright held up a hand. 'Now just hold on a minute, Lee. I'm taking my herd into Smith's Hole for the winter. Now maybe if these two men are gone, we won't have any trouble, but I'm not sure. There is a third man named Dan Matson who is a local leader. He might make trouble for us. Leave him until the last, Sparks. If the Hole men take my offer and get out, I see no reason to eliminate Matson. I'll get word to you in Baggs about Matson.'

Jackson stared blankly at Albright, unable for a moment to fully comprehend what the cowman was saying. He'd had the impression that Carter and Willets were being removed because they were tough hands who would fight as long as they could hold a gun. Since they were wanted men, no one was going to get worked up about their deaths, but Matson was a respectable cattleman who had lived in the Hole for years and, as far as Jackson knew, had never broken a law in his life.

Sparks did not say another word, but turned to the door and opened it. If he could make fifteen hundred dollars instead of a thousand while he was in the Hole, he would do it, Jackson thought. He cried out, 'No. Not Dan Matson. Killing him would get us into real trouble. He ain't like Carter and Willets . . .'

'We'll see,' Albright said.

Sparks spun around and pinned his gaze on Jackson for the first time as if only then aware that another man was in the room. He said, 'Stay out of my way.' He went out and closed the door behind him.

'For God's sake, Mr. Albright,' Jackson said angrily, 'you can't do this. Removing outlaws is one thing, but a man like Dan Matson . . .'

'I know, Lee,' Albright said as if being tolerant of a rebellious child, 'I know exactly how you feel, but I aim to smash all resistance in the Hole so there will be no trouble when

89

the herd is driven in. Now you will not be involved. I asked you and the judge to come here to meet Kurt Sparks and to know what we're planning, but your real job is to get the cattle into the Hole. Of course, if there is any fighting, you'll have to do your part, but I don't anticipate any trouble once these men are taken care of.'

'But with Matson it's just plain murder,' Jackson said, his sense of outrage growing. 'He's a decent man. I tell you the grass in Smith's Hole ain't worth it. I don't savvy how you can stand here and pay a back-shooting bastard like Kurt Sparks to murder Dan Matson.'

'He's had his chance to sell and move out of the Hole the same as the others,' Verling said quickly. 'If he stays to fight, he'll get what's coming to him.'

'But damn it, he hasn't got it coming,' Jackson shouted. 'I tell you . . .'

He stopped, his eyes on Albright. He saw a man transformed, a man who had been outwardly self-controlled and courteous suddenly being possessed of insane fury. It was in his eyes, in the way the corners of his mouth twitched, even in the trembling tips of his fingers.

Albright turned his back to Jackson and stood at the window again looking down into the lighted street below him, his fingers laced behind him. He said in a high-pitched voice, 'I

90

don't need you, Jackson. I can buy a dozen ramrods who are better men than you are. Now get out of here before I kill you.'

Verling took Jackson's arm and led him to the door. He whispered, 'Where are you staying?'

Jackson told him and Verling said, 'I'll see you in a little while.'

Verling opened the door and pushed Jackson into the hall and closed the door. For a moment Lee Jackson stood staring at the door, his heart pounding. He had been fired, and then he wondered why he had tried to argue with Albright. He had known he couldn't change him. Still, he had never seen the Skull owner go out of his head as he had just done, but then he had never known Albright to bargain for the murder of three men as casually as if he were ordering three steers to be butchered.

Jackson walked along the hall to the elevator, thinking that he had solved his problem without intending to. He would return to Smith's Hole, talk Margo into marrying him, and they'd go to North Park. Then he wondered how he had ever found the courage to stand there and shout at Justin Albright the way he had. He guessed he'd been out of his head, too.

Later when he was in his room, the old doubt returned, the old arguments against starting out on his own. Maybe Margo

91

wouldn't many him. He had to have more money than he had saved. He had to keep his job until spring.

Perhaps if he apologized to Albright he would get his job back. He could make out with the additional wages he would earn between now and next summer. He could save nearly all of it. He had never been a man to blow his money on whiskey or women, and his gambling had always been for fun and low stakes.

He sat down on his bed and held his head in his hands. He saw himself for what he was. He hated the mental image that came to him of a weak man who could not make a decision and stick to it, a man who would let himself be involved with murder just to hold a job that gave him the only security he had.

He could not find any real security within himself; he did not really believe in his ability to make a living out of the small North Park spread he intended to buy, and maybe, he told himself bitterly, he didn't really want the responsibility of having a wife and family.

No, that wasn't right. The indecision that had gripped him for so long was a thing of the past. He saw clearly what he had to do. Dan Matson had whipped him, but Dan Matson had also saved his life. If he, Lee Jackson, let events take their projected course, Dan Matson would die with Kurt Sparks' bullet in his back, and Jackson would be as guilty of the murder as Sparks was. He could not, he told himself, let it come to that.

A knock on the door brought him upright. He crossed the room, opened the door, and motioned for Judge Verling to come in. He closed the door, not knowing what Verling would say and at the moment not caring. He had reached a decision, and by God, this was one he would keep. Dan Matson was going to hear what was being planned for him.

Verling sat down in the only chair in the room and heaved a long sigh as if he were too tired to take another breath. He said, 'Well, Lee, you just about cooked your goose. What got into you?'

'Dan Matson saved my life the last time I was in the Hole,' Jackson said. 'I ain't aiming to let Albright murder him.'

'You'll let him,' Verling said, 'and I'll tell you why. You've sold your soul to the devil just like I have and Orly Hunt has and some other men I can name, the devil being Justin Albright. He's insane. You saw that tonight. He thinks he's God. I've seen it before. Someday somebody is going to kill him. Maybe it'll be one of his own men. That will free the rest of us, but until that happens, no one opposes anything that Justin Albright has decided to do.'

He took a cigar out of his pocket, bit off the end, and touched a match flame to the tip. Jackson sat down on the bed. He said, 'Maybe

I did sell my soul, but I figure I bought it back tonight when he fired me.'

'You're a damned fool,' Verling said wearily. 'I talked like a good fellow and got back your job for you. Albright doesn't know it maybe, but he needs you, and I figure you need him as long as he owns Skull and will give you a job.'

'I can make out on my own,' Jackson said firmly. 'I've got some savings. I'm going to get married and buy a spread I've got my eyes on in North Park.'

'He won't let you,' Verling said. 'You ought to know that. He never forgives a man who quits him. He'll let you keep your job, but he's sure as hell going to watch every move you make or don't make from now on. You'd better get that herd into the Hole and bring it out in top shape next spring or you will get fired for good.'

'It's none of his business if I buy a spread . . .'

'He'll make it his business,' Verling said. 'Sometimes you act like you don't know the man. I do or I'd have been shut of him years ago. Orly Hunt knows him. He blackmails you, Lee. He'd ruin you if you left him. He's got the power to do it and he'll use that power in whatever way he needs it. You saw that tonight. Murder is one tool he's used and he's just as indifferent to it as he is when his bank forecloses on a man's spread. He'd get at you in one way or another. Don't you savvy that,

Lee? We belong to him and he never lets any of us go. It's the reason he's got as big as he is. We're slaves. He's used us and other men to build his empire.'

Jackson stood up and looked down at Verling, and for the first time felt sorry for this old, beaten man, and for the first time, felt proud of himself. He said, 'Judge, maybe he's got enough on you and Orly Hunt and other men like you to blackmail you, but he ain't got a damned thing on me, and by God, I ain't his slave and I'm going to live my own life the way I want to.'

And at that moment Lee Jackson believed what he said.

CHAPTER THIRTEEN

Margo Lane could not sleep. She had not slept well for several nights. Nearly a week ago she had maneuvered Dan Matson into saying he would marry her. That had been exactly what she had wanted, but he hadn't been back since.

If he really loved her, if he really wanted to marry her, he'd have found time to call on her during the week. He couldn't be so busy that he was tied up on his piddling little Two Bar every minute of the day and evening for almost a week.

Sure, he would tell her he was too busy to

make the ride to her place, but she knew that wasn't true. It just wasn't that far. A man makes time, she told herself, to do what he considers important, and he certainly had not considered it important to see the girl he had said he wanted to marry.

She struck a match and looked at the clock. Two in the morning! She blew the match out and lay back in bed, her eyes closed. She was so tired of teaching, so tired of living by herself. She wanted a man to take care of her, a family, a real home which she had never known even as a child.

Her father had died when she was a baby. Her mother had worked so hard to raise her that she'd died when Margo was fourteen. She'd been on her own since then. Well, she was better off than some women. At least she had not been forced into a whorehouse. She hadn't had to work every waking hour every day doing housework which some women had to do just to have a place to sleep and a roof over their heads.

No, she wasn't as bad off as some women, but still she was tired, tired, tired. Sometimes when she stopped to think about it, she realized that marriage might mean exchanging one hard and disagreeable life for another.

She might even be worse off with half a dozen kids and a husband to keep house for, but it would be a better life than this. She was sure of that. People respected a woman who was a wife and mother, but they always ridiculed an old maid. The way she was going, that was exactly what she was going to be.

Of course, there was always Lee Jackson. In time he'd get around to marrying her. She did not doubt that he loved her or that he meant it when he said he wanted to marry her, but that would be settling for the worst kind of marriage. He'd buy the little spread in North Park he'd talked about, but it would be mortgaged and he'd be trying to pay it off all of his life. He'd need money to buy a good bull, or barbed wire, or shingles for the roof.

She remembered the place very well and how rundown the house and barn were. No, marrying Dan Matson would be a better deal for her. He wasn't rich, but his house was comfortable, he had a small herd, his spread was paid for, and she knew there would be money enough for a new dress now and then, or even a trip to Denver.

Then she began to cry. She had done everything she could to get Dan to marry her except go to bed with him. She'd do that, too, if it would get the right result, but she was afraid to make an overt offer. It would offend him, and she had never been able to work out a situation where it just seemed the natural and proper thing to do.

She laughed hysterically when the word 'proper' came into her mind. She had a notion that going to bed with Dan would never seem proper to him unless they were married. Morals were no problem to her, but they were to Dan. Even if she got herself pregnant and forced Dan to marry her, she would have made a bad bargain for herself. She had seen it happen too many times.

No, somehow she had to make Dan *want* to marry her. She thought she had accomplished it last Saturday when he'd left and she'd felt good about her future. It was the first time he had said he wanted to marry her and she had believed him, but now she did not feel the confidence she had felt when he'd left. She had expected to see him Sunday, but he hadn't come. She had expected to see him every evening, but still he hadn't come.

Tomorrow was Saturday again. He'd be here then, of course. Along with the rest of the men, he would be cutting dead cedars and piling them on top of Lone Rock for a signal fire when the Skull herd was discovered on its way into the Hole.

She was taking a pot of beans and a pie to the supper at the schoolhouse. She would see him then. He might even stop to see her on his way to Lone Rock, but that wasn't good enough. She wanted him to make the ride here just to see her and for no other reason.

Sometimes she thought that Dan was in love with Bess Bailey, though it didn't seem reasonable. She didn't know why she thought that, unless it was the way he always defended

Bess if Margo made a critical remark about her. Or maybe it was because Dan, knowing he could have Margo any time he said, was not showing the proper interest. If there was another woman, it had to be Bess. There weren't any other single women in the Hole.

Well, she'd have it out with Dan the next time she saw him. Either he was going to ...

A noise in front of the cabin brought her upright in bed. She was sure she had heard a horse, but why would anybody be riding past this time of the night? She put her feet on the floor, cocking her head to listen, and a moment later she heard the crack of heels on boards and the jingling of spurs as a man stepped up on the porch and crossed to the door.

When he knocked, she struck a match and lighted a lamp, then pulled on her robe. She picked up the lamp and carried it to the door, uneasy because she could think of no reason that would bring anyone calling at this time of night. For a moment she hesitated, holding the lamp in one hand, the other hand gripping the doorknob.

The knock came again. She called, 'Who is it?'

'Lee.'

She jerked the door open and saw that it was indeed Lee Jackson. 'Come in,' she cried. 'What are you riding around this time of night for?'

He pulled the screen door open and stepped inside, not attempting to answer until he had dropped into the nearest chair. She saw that he had not shaved for a week, that he was dead tired, and for a moment she wondered if he was running from someone, if his life was in danger and he was coming to her for help. She backed away and set the lamp on the table, thinking that she didn't want to get involved in any of his troubles.

He wiped a hand across his face. He said, 'I'm here to ask you to do something for me. I don't figure I can do it, hating Dan Matson like I do, but I owe him a favor.'

It took Margo a moment to fully comprehend what he had said. She knew very well that Lee Jackson and Dan Matson hated each other. Now, for Lee to want to do Dan a favor, well, that was hard to believe. Wanting her to do it for him was even harder to believe.

Then she thought: *It would give me a chance to see Dan without him thinking I was chasing him.*

'Of course I'll do whatever you ask, Lee,' she said. 'You know that.'

He shook his head. 'I dunno, Margo. Maybe you'd do it for Matson. I ain't sure you'd do it for me.'

'I don't like what you're saying,' she said sharply. 'You have no right to even think it. If I'm going to marry you, I can certainly do you a favor.'

'If you are going to marry me,' he said wearily, then made a motion as if to wipe out the conversation and start over. 'All right, Margo. All right.'

'You want anything to eat?' she asked. 'I can start a fire and make some coffee.'

He shook his head. 'No, I ain't got much time. There's a man in camp named Orly Hunt who's kind o' keeping an eye on me. I'm hoping to get back without him knowing where I've been.' He swallowed, then asked, 'Have you seen a stranger in the Hole? A big man, dark-skinned, with a long nose?'

She shook her head. 'No, I haven't seen any stranger. Not since the sheriff was here a few days ago.'

'He'll be here,' Jackson said. 'He's aiming to shoot Matson. He'll plug Lige Carter and Nate Willets, too, but I don't give a damn about them. They're wanted men. It's different with Matson. I'm asking you to warn him. I don't cotton to him, seeing as he licked hell out of me, but he don't deserve a shot in the back, neither.'

Margo's hand came up to her throat. She knew she had heard Jackson correctly, but the idea that Dan would be murdered was too much. She had always considered him as being as indestructible as Lone Rock or the walls of Maroon canyon.

'Why, Lee?' she demanded. 'Dan hasn't hurt anyone. Why would they kill him?'

101

'Because he'll make trouble for Justin Albright,' Jackson said. 'If you tell anybody what I've told you, chances are I'll get shot in the back, too. Just give Matson the warning, but don't tell him how you heard it or who told you.'

He rose and stood looking at her, waiting for her promise. She said, 'Of course, Lee. I won't tell him.'

For a moment Jackson didn't speak, his hungry eyes on her as if trying to picture her so sharply that he would remember exactly how she looked after he had left her. He said finally, 'Margo, I'm quitting Albright. It's getting too thick for me. I figured I had to go on working for him until this trouble was over, but now I know I don't. To hell with him.'

He paused as if thinking about why he had changed his mind, then he added slowly, 'It was just pride, I guess, not wanting anybody to know I was afraid of a fight, but I know him a little better, too well to fight for him He ain't human, Margo. He's a . . . a monster, the kind you have in your nightmares. That's why I'm quitting him. I'm going to buy that spread in North Park. Now, like you wanted me to. Will you marry me when I get it?'

'Yes, Lee,' she whispered. 'Yes.'

He kissed her, holding her hard against him, his lips bruising hers with their urgency, then he swung around and walked out, so tired his shoulders slumped. She watched him until he disappeared into the darkness, but she wasn't really seeing him. Her mind was on Dan Matson.

She would give Dan the warning early in the morning. She would save his life. She would point that out to him and he would be in debt to her. He was an honorable man who would meet his obligations. He would marry her. He wouldn't feel right unless he did.

CHAPTER FOURTEEN

Dan Matson had finished his morning chores and was saddling his buckskin when he heard a rider coming in on the road from Bald Rock. Stepping around his horse, he saw that it was a woman. A moment later he recognized Margo Lane.

Dan swore. Right now the last person he wanted to see was Margo. He had been torn all week between wanting to see her and rebelling against his agreement to marry her. He still wasn't sure how he felt about her. He had doubts and he guessed that was enough to make him shy off.

If a man really loved a girl, he wouldn't worry about his doubts. Now she'd probably come to nag him about not seeing her all week. She had reason to be sore about it, but he didn't want to be nagged about anything.

He was very much aware that she wanted to get married now. Well, he wasn't going to be hurried. If she as much as opened her mouth . . .

She was there then, slipping out of the saddle and running to him. She cried, 'There's a man coming to kill you. You've got to leave the country.'

She had been crying. She put her hands on his arms and tried to shake him when he stared blankly at her. 'Don't you understand, Dan? Albright is sending an assassin to murder you. He knows that you're the only man who can make the Hole men fight. Without you they'll pull out and Albright won't have any trouble getting the grass he wants.'

It got through to him then. He demanded, 'Now where did you hear a cock 'n' bull story like that?'

'Never mind where I heard it,' she snapped. 'He's a big man, dark-skinned, with a long nose. He's probably somewhere in the Hole now. If he isn't, he soon will be, so you don't have much time. You've got to get out now.'

'I don't believe it,' he said. 'Albright is a lot of things and he'll do about anything to get the Hole grass, but hiring a dry gulcher is more 'n even Justin Albright would do. I asked you where you heard it?'

'I promised not to tell.' Her fingers dug deeper into his arms. 'All I can tell you is that it's true. This man is supposed to kill Carter

104

and Willets, too, but they're both outlaws. You're the one who's important. I'll go with you, Dan. Anywhere! Just so you're safe. All I want is for you to stay alive.'

He stared thoughtfully at her, realizing that if he were eliminated along with Carter and Willets, Albright would indeed get his grass without any great trouble. He could see, too, that murdering Willets and Carter might not cut much ice with most people, including Sheriff Buck Douglas. Folks would say that it was good riddance and shrug their shoulders, that they'd been afraid of the two men all the time they had been here.

Knocking off Dan Matson was something else. He belonged in the Hole and most of the other ranchers looked to him for leadership. There would be no resistance if the dry gulcher got him. Then he shook his head. No, he couldn't believe that Albright would go that far. Buck Douglas might overlook Willets' and Carter's murders, but he couldn't overlook Dan Matson's killing, and the trail would eventually lead to Albright.

He shook his head. 'You know I can't just tuck my tail between my legs and run. I wouldn't even if I could. Anyhow, I still don't believe what you're saying. I might if I knew who you heard it from.'

She bit her lip, hesitating. Finally she said, 'Please don't tell anybody, Dan. I promised him I wouldn't tell. Lee Jackson woke me up in the middle of the night to tell me. He asked me to warn you.'

'Jackson?' Dan laughed. 'Well now, that makes good sense, don't it? Can't you see why he told you that? He figures it'll booger me into pulling my freight and that would be as good as killing me and a hell of a lot less dangerous to Albright.'

He shook his head again. 'No, that's a smart notion Jackson had, and you sucked into it. I'll stay, Margo. If Jackson starts pushing that herd down Maroon canyon, he's gonna be in more trouble than he ever dreamed about. You tell him that the next time you see him.'

She stepped back, her arms dropping to her sides. 'I love you, Dan. All I'm trying to do is to keep you alive. You can't fight a man who hides in the rocks and shoots you when you don't even know he's anywhere around.' She motioned toward the east rim. 'He might be up there right now drawing a bead on you. Can't you understand that, Dan?'

'Oh, I understand it, all right,' he said, 'but it ain't gonna happen. Now you mount up and git for home. We're cutting cedars today. Willets and Carter will be along pretty soon. We're gonna be hungry by sundown. You go home and bake some pies and fry a couple of chickens. I'll see you tonight at the schoolhouse.'

She stood frozen, staring at him. Tears ran down her cheeks as she stamped her foot.

'Dan Matson, you are impossible. Just impossible.' She whirled away from him, mounted, and rode back the way she had come.

He watched her for a time, frowning thoughtfully, then glanced uneasily at the rim. There was, as he had told Laura Bailey a week ago, a good chance that somebody would try to bushwhack him from the rim, but it was too long a shot for even a sharpshooter to be accurate. He glanced at the river, thinking that was a better bet for a dry gulcher. A man could hide in the willows and be close enough to kill him any time that he was in the open around his house or barn.

A prickle ran down his spine. He still couldn't believe that Albright would stoop to murder, but the man was capable of anything, and anything included murder. Still, it seemed more reasonable that Jackson had told Margo what he had, thinking that it would scare him out of the Hole. After all, Jackson was about the last man in the state of Colorado who would try to save his life.

He finished tightening the cinch, his mind going back to his fight with Jackson in Charley Klein's saloon. He remembered what Willets and Carter had said and he was sure they would have killed Jackson if he hadn't ordered the man kept alive for Douglas to talk to.

A bullet was Willets' and Carter's way of solving such a problem. He wasn't sure

107

whether Jackson had been conscious enough to know what was happening or not. If he had, maybe this was his way of repaying what he considered to be a debt. Jackson was on the wrong side, but he was an honorable man, and he would probably try to repay Dan for saving his life if he knew what had happened.

So the uneasiness grew in Dan no matter how hard he tried to reason it away. Margo was right about one thing. You couldn't fight a dry gulcher. He guessed that was about the only thing he was really afraid of. A man couldn't fight a ghost, and that was just about the same thing as fighting anyone he couldn't see.

He got his ax from behind his house, mounted, and started toward Bald Rock. Glancing back, he saw Carter and Willets coming and reined up to wait for them. He had not talked to either since the night they had held him and Sheriff Douglas under their guns, so he was a little nervous about what they would say and do.

A moment later he saw that he had nothing to worry about. Both men greeted him as naturally as if nothing had happened. He had always got along well with them, neighboring with them and exchanging work with them more than with anyone else in the Hole because his spread was next to theirs and they were the only ranchers in the north end.

He reined in beside them, Carter asking,

'You figger the old bastard's about to make a move?'

'Just about,' Dan said.

He considered telling them what Margo had said, and decided against it. He didn't think they would scare easily and pull out, but he didn't want to take any chances. There wouldn't be much of a fight without them. That thought upset him. Jackson just might be telling the truth, the uneasiness working into his mind again.

To hell with it, he thought. They'd play it out with the hand they'd been dealt and hope that Jackson was bluffing. A few minutes later they reached the Bailey ranch. Bess was in the yard. She waved and called, 'Wait up, Dan.'

Carter snickered. 'She wants to ride with you, Dan. You reckon Margo's making her jealous? Maybe you've been spending too much time with the teacher.'

'Go to hell,' Dan said amiably. 'Wait for me at the schoolhouse.'

'Sure,' Willets said. 'We ain't so anxious to swing an ax that we're gonna hurry right on up to Lone Rock without you.'

Dan reined toward Bess, irritated by her interference. To his way of thinking it would be better if Bess would wait and go with her mother to the schoolhouse later in the day, but no, she was dressed in men's clothes as usual. She'd tag along to Lone Rock and chop wood with the best of them.

Bess picked up her ax and was in the saddle by the time he reached her. She said, 'You don't mind me riding with you, do you, Dan? I've got a question to ask.'

'Come along,' he said. 'Ask away.'

She rode beside him for a time, frowning as if not sure how she should word her question, then she blurted, 'Just what did that little tart want with you this morning?'

'Margo?' He glanced at Bess, curious about why she had asked the question. 'You jealous?'

'Jealous?' Bess cried indignantly. 'Hell no. Why should I be jealous? I just wanted to know why that floozy got up so early in the morning to see you.'

'It makes me sore for you to call her a tart and a floozy,' Dan said angrily. 'She's neither as far as I know. She wanted to save my life. You can't fault her for that.'

'Oh.' Bess stared straight ahead. 'Maybe you'd better explain that. I can think of some things Margo could do for you, but saving your life ain't one of them.'

'She thought she was,' Dan said. 'She had word that Albright was sending a dry gulcher into the Hole to ambush me along with Carter and Willets.'

Bess stiffened and was silent for a moment, then she said, 'For once she might be right. I've wondered if Albright would do something like that.'

'I think she was passing along a bluff just

110

like Albright hoped she would,' Dan said. 'He wants to scare me into running.'

'Have you told Carter and Willets?'

'No, I didn't want to worry them,' Dan said. 'I was afraid they might slope out of here if they heard it. I just don't believe it.'

'I do,' Bess said somberly. 'Maybe all three of you ought to get out of the Hole. I can't stand the thought of Albright having his way, but I don't want you dead.' She glanced at him and looked away quickly. 'Or the other two, either.'

She had quarreled with him ever since her father had died, sometimes over such trivial matters that the row had seemed ridiculous. He had often thought that she would have been happier if he were dead and not around for her to quarrel with. Now he sensed genuine concern for him. He wondered about it because it wasn't at all like the Bess Bailey he had known for the last few years.

He decided not to press her and changed the subject with, 'Looks like it'll be a good day for woodcutting.'

'A fine day,' she agreed gravely.

After that they rode in silence until they reached the schoolhouse.

CHAPTER FIFTEEN

Lee Jackson reached camp before sunup. He had hoped to get in before Orly Hunt was awake, but he found Hunt hunkered beside the fire drinking coffee. He said, 'You're riding late, Lee. Or early, whichever it is.'

Jackson poured a cup of coffee and squatted beside Hunt. 'You keeping an eye on me?'

'You can say that. I'm supposed to be Justin Albright's personal representative until we have the Hole grass.' He shot a glance at Jackson. 'I figure you've been down into the Hole.'

'Well?'

'The boss wouldn't like that,' Hunt said. 'He don't trust you worth a damn. Not since you bucked him about rubbing Dan Matson out. It's like the judge told you. Albright figgers you're for him or against him, and he ain't got no middle ground for you to walk on.'

Jackson remembered that Hunt had been gone from camp all of one day and most of one night earlier in the week. At the time he had wondered if Hunt had ridden into Craig to see Judge Verling. Now he was certain that was what the man had done.

He said, 'You seem to know quite a bit about me and Albright.'

'I had a talk with the judge,' Hunt said, 'which same you've probably guessed. I don't care for Albright's methods no more 'n you do, but as long as I'm working for him, I'll go along with them methods.'

'Including murder?'

Hunt nodded. 'Including murder.' He tossed the coffee grounds from his cup into the fire, adding, 'I reckon every man has his breaking-off point as to what his conscience will let him do. I can think of some things Albright would do if he had to that would make me get to hell out of here, but hiring Kurt Sparks ain't one of them.'

'Murdering Dan Matson is mine,' Jackson said. 'I've been fighting myself all week until I finally decided it was time for me to do something I was proud of. I left word in the Hole that Sparks was coming.'

'I figgered that was what you'd been up to,' Hunt said angrily, 'and I say you're a damned fool for coming back here. Albright will skin you and hang your hide up to dry.'

Jackson was silent for a time, his brooding gaze on the fire. Funny thing, he thought, how a man's conscience works. He could not remain silent and let Sparks dry gulch Matson, but he couldn't bring himself to ride off yet, leaving his job and whatever security was still here, yet he knew that Hunt was right. He could not go on working for Albright. He wouldn't have a job the minute the Skull

113

owner heard what he had done.

'I'm aiming to quit in a few days,' Jackson said finally. 'I've told you I want to marry the schoolteacher and buy a spread in North Park. I just ain't ready to go yet.'

'Marry the girl if you want to,' Hunt said, 'and then take her a long ways from here. I've told you and the judge told you that Albright don't forget and he don't forgive. Sure, he took you back for a few days, mostly so he could watch you through me, but you won't be working for him much longer whether I tell him what you done or not.'

'It's no skin off his nose if I settle in North Park,' Jackson said angrily.

'He'll make it his skin,' Hunt said. 'He's got a dozen ways of getting at you. Through the bank. Or he can cut off your credit at any store where you were trading. He's got a spread on the Canadian, as you know, so he's got riders in North Park and that means you'll start losing stock.' He shook his head. 'Go away, Lee. A long ways from here.'

'I've got a few days yet,' Jackson said stubbornly. 'It'll be about a week before we ease the herd downstream until we're close to the top of Maroon canyon. That'll be the time for me to quit. You've got the money to pay me, haven't you? You've got it for Sparks.'

Hunt nodded. 'I've got it, but today is the time for you to quit. Damn it, I wish I could get it through your thick skull that Albright will hound you till you're dead if you hang around here.'

'You don't like him no more 'n I do,' Jackson said. 'How come you keep on working for him?'

'I told you,' Hunt said sourly. 'I've got a living for the rest of my life if I do what he tells me to.'

'It's more 'n that, ain't it?' Jackson said. 'The judge said that him and you and men like you belong to Albright, that you're his slaves.'

'That's about the size of it,' Hunt admitted, his tone still sour. 'I take orders or I go to prison.'

'Looks like you don't have a breaking-off point,' Jackson said.

'Oh, I've got one, all right,' Hunt said. 'Some things Albright would do that I wouldn't stand for. I'd go to prison if it came to that.'

'Like what?'

'Killing a woman, for one thing,' Hunt answered. 'Or a child. Both could happen once you get a war like this started.' He shrugged. 'But it would be an accident if it happened, though I figger Albright wouldn't balk at killing either a woman or a kid if they stood in his way.'

'As long as he didn't pull the trigger.'

Hunt nodded. 'Anyhow, there ain't no women or kids in his way on this deal.'

'Maybe Laura Bailey,' Jackson said. 'Or her

115

girl Bess. He tried to frame 'em with your help.'

'Just a scare maneuver,' Hunt said. 'They'll leave the Hole with the rest of 'em once Matson is out of the way.' He rose and tossed his cigarette stub into the fire. 'I'll tell you something, Lee. If you don't get out now, you'll wind up in the Hole fighting for Matson and the rest of 'em if Matson is still alive. That ain't gonna make no friends on either side. I read about a man named Benedict Arnold who sold his saddle. The British didn't like him, either.'

Hunt walked away. Jackson stared at the man's back in the thin morning light wondering what Hunt had done that gave Albright the power to send him to prison. And how could Hunt's conscience distinguish between murdering Dan Matson and a woman? The way Jackson saw it, murder was murder, and then he found himself choking on his own logic. He hadn't been bothered when Albright hired Sparks to murder Willets and Carter. Every man lives by his standards, he told himself. Maybe his were no higher than Orly Hunt's.

The cook banged the triangle and the crew moved in for breakfast. That was when Kurt Sparks rode up from the east. Jackson saw him coming and recognized him before he reined to a stop. This was Orly Hunt's business, not his, so he stayed in the background, letting

Sparks play it his way.

It was plain that Sparks didn't want to involve Jackson any more than Jackson wanted to be involved. He ignored him, asking for Orly Hunt.

'That's me,' Hunt said, walking toward the man. 'Get down and have some breakfast.'

Sparks shook his head. 'I et earlier. I just wanted to talk to you.'

Hunt nodded and moved away from the fire, Sparks following. Jackson and the others watched them curiously. Later, after Sparks had left, riding toward Maroon creek, Hunt said to Jackson, 'He wants three good horses left at certain points on the road between here and Baggs.'

'Why?'

'He didn't say, but it's my guess he wants 'em to make a fast ride between here and Baggs where he'll make sure he's seen after he knocks off a couple of 'em. I've heard about that bastard. He's good at a lot of things, including riding. He'll make a ride that nobody will believe.'

'All right,' Jackson said. 'Pick out your horses. I reckon you'll be gone a day or so.'

Hunt nodded. 'He wants me to be in Baggs to identify him.'

'You tell him I passed the word that he was coming?'

A grin curled Hunt's lips. 'No sir, I did not, and I ain't going to. I figger that's his business,

117

not mine.'

'Thanks,' Jackson said.

'Well, I didn't want him to beef you right here in front of me. Sooner or later he'll get to you if you're still around. He's bound to hear. Or guess.'

'You figure he's got a breaking-off point?'

Hunt shrugged. 'I don't know as to that, but Albright has several. He wouldn't cheat at cards. He wouldn't take your money at the point of a gun. He wouldn't rape a woman.'

Later, after Jackson had saddled a horse and was riding out to the herd that was drifting west along the south bank of the Little Snake, it struck him again that every man dances to his own tune. How could a man order a woman's murder, when raping her was something he could not do? Or rob the Hole ranchers of their grass, when he could not take a man's money at the point of a gun?

Then he put it out of his mind, telling himself that it was Justin Albright's problem to live with his own conscience. Then his thoughts turned to Margo Lane, the softness of her body, the sweetness of her lips, and how it would be to sleep with her.

He realized, then, that it was his own weakness that had held him back with her, his nagging need to have more money in the bank, to go on working for Albright as long as he could, his inability to make decisions. Well, that was past.

Sometime between now and the end of the week he would see Margo and set the date for their wedding if she would have him. He would not allow her to postpone the date. He'd had enough. He would buy the North Park spread regardless of Orly Hunt's warning. Then he wondered why he had decided to wait until later in the week. He could not find any answer to that question.

He rode with his long shadow before him, his lungs filled with the clear, winey air of the desert. Suddenly he felt proud of himself. He would not wait until the end of the week to speak to Margo. He would do it as soon as Hunt returned from Baggs.

Then, with his thoughts running wild and free as they never had before, another question came to him. Why hadn't Hunt told Sparks about him informing the Hole people that the dry gulcher was coming? The answer came to him at once. Orly Hunt was a slave and a slave was never a completely loyal man. Justin Albright was whipped unless he came to personally lead the Skull cowboys when they attacked the Hole ranchers. If Albright had any notion of possible defeat, he'd be here.

CHAPTER SIXTEEN

When Kurt Sparks reached the base of Lone Rock in Maroon canyon, he heard something above him from the rim which he could not identify over the rustle of the stream and the sound of his horse's hoofs on the sandstone trail.

He reined up, cocking his head to listen. He was always a cautious man. If he hadn't been, he would not have lived as long as he had. Men were up there, a good-sized bunch of them from the volume of talk, but the distance was too great to make out any words. Then he heard the clear, echoing ring of ax on wood. He rode on, wondering about it but deciding it didn't concern him.

When he reached the bottom of the grade and came out of the canyon, he noticed something else that struck him as being strange at a time when everyone should be worried about keeping his home. Several women were laying boards across saw horses for tables beside the schoolhouse. It was a hot day, but smoke was pouring from the chimney of the teacherage, so they were cooking, probably having some kind of community celebration. This, too, he decided, had nothing to do with him or his mission here.

He had never been in Smith's Hole before,

but he had talked to a man in Baggs about it and he knew what to expect. It was not much different from other settlements he had seen in the cattle country, isolated by geography so that it had become largely self-sufficient. For that reason the people had learned to look after themselves and to seldom call the sheriff or a doctor or a preacher for help.

They would fight for what they considered theirs. Justin Albright knew this, of course, but he also knew that if he took out a few key men, the rest of the people would run like sheep. This thought gave great satisfaction to Sparks and brought something that was close to a smile to his lips. That was the reason men like Albright employed him. He would have such employment as long as similar isolated communities existed and there were cowmen like Albright who made their own laws.

He felt comfortable with the thought that he would never be out of work because there would always be communities like Smith's Hole and there would always be cowmen as greedy and unscrupulous as Justin Albright. In fact, his immediate future was taken care of. He was going from here to Wyoming, and from there to Montana.

He had been told that there were only three buildings in Bald Rock: the schoolhouse, the teacherage, and the combination store, post office, and saloon. He rode toward the latter, his gaze swinging from the cliffs to the south that marked the edge of the Hole to the ridges on the north that blocked out his view in that direction. He could not see beyond them, but he judged there were other ranches that were not visible from here.

He noted the good grass, much of it stirrup high, and he understood why Albright was making his move. It meant the difference next spring between a fat steer and a lean one. He saw two groups of ranch buildings to the north that lay between him and the ridges, several more to the south and at least three across the river.

Sparks tied in front of the saloon and went in. An old man who was sitting at a poker table rose and moved behind the bar, asking, 'What'll it be, mister?'

'Whiskey,' Sparks said.

The old man poured his drink and shoved it across the rough pine bar. Sparks tossed a coin on the bar, saying, 'Seems purty quiet. Don't nobody live around here?'

'Oh, sure,' the old man answered. 'A dozen families or so. The men are on the rim above Maroon canyon cutting wood today for a signal fire and some of the women are in the schoolhouse fixing tonight's supper. I reckon the rest of the women will be there before evening.'

Sparks rolled the glass between his fingers, asking, 'Now what in the hell would men in a place like this want a signal fire for? You got some wild Injuns around here?'

'White Injuns, I guess, if you want to call 'em that,' the old man said. 'I reckon you've rode in from a long ways off, or you'd know that a grabby son of a bitch named Justin Albright is figgering on stealing our grass. We aim to set that fire to going when his herd starts moving this way and he'll run into some trouble when the boys get together.'

'No, I hadn't heard about this Albright gent, but I did ride quite a piece this morning and yesterday. I've got a horse ranch north of Casper. I heard there were some horses for sale down here. I've got most of what I want at a ranch over on Fortification creek, but I'm in the market for a few more.'

'There ain't no horses for sale hereabouts,' the barman said. 'I'd have heard about it if there was. I figger you had your ride for nothing, mister.'

'I'll see a couple of men before I go back,' Sparks said, 'just to be sure. I was told that Lige Carter and Nate Willets raised horses.'

'Naw.' The old man shook his head. 'Not for sale, I mean. They raise some horses, all right, but they sell to a liveryman in Craig. You won't do no business with them.'

'No harm dickering,' Sparks said. 'Where'll I find them?'

'Right now they're up on Lone Rock cutting wood with everybody else. I'd be there, too, but I'm so old and crippled up I ain't no good any more.'

'Where's their spreads?' Sparks asked. 'I'll go look at their horses. If they ain't what I want, I won't even stop to dicker. I'll just turn around and ride back.'

The old man shrugged. 'I tell you there ain't no use, but it's your time and trouble, I reckon. You can't see their outfits from here, but if you ride north over a couple of humps, you'll see 'em. Their cabins ain't more 'n a hundred yards apart.'

'I could see two outfits from here to the north,' Sparks said. 'You sure they ain't the ones?'

'By God, I oughtta know,' the old man said angrily. 'You don't seem to believe nothing I say. I've lived here since Hec was a pup and I know every ranch and family in Smith's Hole. The first one is the Bailey place. Just two women live there, Laura Bailey and her girl Bess. On past it is Dan Matson's spread. He lives alone and he ain't got no horses to sell, neither.'

'Thanks,' Sparks said.

He swallowed his drink, thinking he was in luck with Willets and Carter living close together. He might get both of them at the same time and be on his way to Baggs as soon as it was dark. Later, when and if he got the word, he'd be back for Matson. Now he knew where his third victim lived.

Sparks strode to the door, then paused and

124

looked back. 'You ain't real smart, trying to tell me I won't buy some horses if I see anything I'd have. I'm a purty good judge of horse flesh and a hell of a good trader when it comes to getting what I want.'

Anger had been festering in the old man and this was all it took to set it off. He screeched, 'Don't tell me I ain't smart, damn you. You're the one with nothing between your ears but pig slop. I know what you'll find up there and I know what Willets and Carter will say.'

Sparks walked back to the bar. He reached across it and, grabbing the old man by the shoulders, dragged him across the pine planks. Sparks shook him until his teeth rattled, then threw him to the floor. He said, 'So I've got nothing but pig slop between my ears, have I? We'll see what's between my ears. We'll see. I figger you're the one with pig slop.'

He kicked the old man in the ribs and wheeled and stalked out of the saloon. The baiman's words had stirred a crazy rage in him that had brought about more than one man's death and now he was tempted to go back and finish this one off. For a moment he stood beside his horse until sanity returned. He was not one to let the sheer pleasure of killing interfere with a killing he was paid to do. He would not let it interfere this time.

He mounted and rode north, noting that the good grass held. He passed the Bailey place, curious about why two women would run a spread by themselves in a country where men always outnumbered the women. He decided they probably had help from their neighbor, Dan Matson.

Chances were that Matson had a good thing going, taking his pay in service at night with one of the women. He had no idea how old a man Matson was, or how old the women were. Sometimes it didn't make much difference about age when it came to bedding down with a woman. The old one might be better than the daughter.

He studied the Matson spread more closely, noting the distance from the rim to the east down to the floor of the Hole. That would be the safest place to be when he earned his last $500, but the distance was great. He was an expert shot with a rifle, but even an expert would have to be lucky to do the job at that distance. He was a tidy man who took pride in his work, and he hated to use more than one bullet per job.

The best place would be from the willows along the river. The only people close enough to hear the shot would be the Bailey women and he had never seen a woman who presented a threat to him. He'd be gone long before the men in the Hole even thought about pursuit.

The drawback was that he'd have to return to the Hole, and after Willets' and Carter's killings all of their neighbors would be on the lookout for strangers. The old man in the saloon could identify him so the alibi he planned to set up in Baggs might not be enough to save him. It wouldn't take a third killing for these people to forget about such things as alibis and trials.

Well, he'd take a look at the Hole from the rim before he decided. A man couldn't really tell by looking up as to how it would be shooting down. He'd stop up there after he came back from Baggs. Now his job was to get Willets and Carter.

He put Matson out of his thoughts and rode on toward the ridge that lay directly ahead, a sense of exhilaration taking possession of him. This feeling always came to him just before and after he killed a man. Today he would kill two men.

CHAPTER SEVENTEEN

They came down from Lone Rock late in the afternoon, a long column of riders led by Dan Matson and Bess Bailey. Every man in the Hole, except Charley Klein, had showed up for work. They had finished the job, leaving a pile of dead cedars ten feet high.

A number of green trees had been thrown on top so that the amount of smoke from the

127

fire would be greater than that made by the dead limbs. Dan was sure that even Nate Willets and Lige Carter would be able to see the smoke from their cabins. If they could, the other ranchers could, too, because Willets and Carter lived farther from Lone Rock than anyone else.

Dan was pleased with the turnout and the way everyone had worked. He had been worried that some of the Hole ranchers would begin talking about selling out to Justin Albright, now that the time he had given them was nearly up, but so far he had heard no talk of quitting.

Instead, he had sensed a stubborn, tight-lipped attitude on everyone's part. For the first time since Albright had made his first threat, Dan was satisfied that the Hole men would hang and rattle. He was well aware that if someone started talking defeat, the rest might suddenly lose their courage. Now, with the deadline only a few days away, he didn't believe it would happen.

They were hungry and tired and thirsty when they reached the schoolhouse and they greeted Laura Bailey's announcement that supper was ready with loud cheers. They tied their horses and made for the pump to wash up.

Margo Lane ran to Dan as soon as he turned from the hitch pole. She gripped his arms just as she had that morning. She whispered, 'He's here, Dan.'

She had been crying and now he saw terror in her eyes. She had always lacked the tough core of courage that Bess Bailey possessed, but this was the first time he had seen such exaggerated fear. He had tried to forget the warning she had given him that morning, and by working hard he had at least partially succeeded. He had always known that fear was contagious and now, in spite of himself, he felt a prickle run down his spine. Instinctively, he glanced up at the rim, then turned his gaze back to Margo.

'How do you know?' he asked.

'I saw him ride by this morning,' she said. 'I was helping Laura Bailey fix the tables when he rode past. He went into the store, stayed a few minutes, and left. He looked just like Lee said he did.' Her grip tightened on his arms. 'He's bad, Dan. I could tell by looking at him.'

He would have laughed if this hadn't been so serious. He had never been able to tell how bad a man was by just looking at him, and he did not believe Margo could, but he understood how it was with her, so he did not challenge her statement.

'Anyone else see him?'

'Laura Bailey did,' Margo answered. 'We were bringing the boards for the table from the schoolhouse when he went by. I had to go to my place to see about some beans I was cooking, so I was inside for a while. When I

129

came out, he was leaving. I don't know what he did. Maybe just bought a drink.'

'Which way did he ride?'

'North,' she said quickly 'Toward your place. Dan, you've got to leave the Hole. He's up there somewhere waiting for you.'

He shook his head. 'I ain't going back over that with you, so quit pushing.'

'Have you told Carter and Willets about him coming?'

'No, but I guess I'd better,' Dan answered. 'Have you seen Charley Klein?'

'No.' She frowned. 'That's kind of funny, now that you mention it. You know how Charley is, always making a nuisance of himself.'

'I've got to wash up,' he said and, jerking away from her, walked toward the pump.

Bess was the next in line when he came up behind her. She turned to him, asking tartly, 'What's our little schoolteacher hanging onto you like a clinging vine for?'

'I told you she said Albright was sending a dry gulcher into the Hole to get me and Lige and Nate,' Dan said. 'Well, she says he's here.'

Bess glanced at him, biting her lip. 'I suppose she wants you to go away with her?'

'She mentioned it.'

'Then I'd say she's lying,' Bess snapped. 'I don't believe there is any dry gulcher.'

'She says your ma saw him, too.'

'The hell she did.' Bess hesitated, then

130

walked toward her mother who had just left the schoolhouse with a pie in each hand. She returned a moment later. 'Margo wasn't lying. At least a stranger rode by here this morning.' She didn't say anything more until she had washed and dried her face and hands, then she asked softly, 'What are you going to do?'

'If Charley don't show up purty quick, I'm going over to the store and see what happened to him.'

Dan pumped a basin of water and washed, the uneasiness in him growing. Margo was right. Charley Klein was a lonely man and he usually did make a nuisance of himself whenever there was a dance or party or community picnic. Normally he was the first to appear and the last to leave.

When Dan joined Margo at the table, he asked, 'Charley ain't showed up all day?'

She shook her head. 'I haven't seen him.'

'I'll eat and then get over there,' he said. He felt guilty for not going now, but the others had started to eat. As he thought about it, he could not find any reason for the killer harming an old man like Charley Klein. Dan had had very little experience with hired killers, so he had no basis for judging what one of them might do or not do.

When he'd been a boy, some of the Wild Bunch had wintered in Smith's Hole, but they'd been bank and train robbers, not hired killers. Actually most of them hadn't even been skilled gunfighters, then he reminded himself that there was no relationship between a gunfighter and a dry gulcher. A man who would face another man with a gun in his hand or holster and one who would shoot his victim in the back were in no way alike.

Now that the thought about it, he guessed he had never seen a paid killer, but it seemed to him that such a man would work at his trade and not be sidetracked by someone or something that was not part of his mission, so probably Charley's absence had nothing to do with the dry gulcher's presence in the Hole.

He was jarred from the run of this thoughts by Margo's question, 'When are you going to tell Willets and Carter?'

He had finished his pie. He said, 'I'll tell 'em as soon as I get back. Right now I'm going over to the store. It just ain't like Charley to not be here.'

He rose and started toward the store, then remembered that they had not worked out a schedule for lookouts on Lone Rock. He wheeled and walked back along the table until he came to Buffalo Jack Roman.

'I'm going over to the store to see what's the matter with Charley,' Dan said. 'It ain't his way to miss a free meal like this.'

Roman looked around, 'Say, you're right. I hadn't even missed the old bastard.'

'If I'm not back in a little while,' Dan said, 'I'll want you to see that there's somebody up there on Lone Rock for the next week.'

'We'll work it out.' Roman promised.

Dan strode to his horse, still unable to grasp the fact that any man, killer or not, would harm an old man who had done nothing to him or was not part of his reason. There was always a possibility that Charley had had a heart attack or simply fallen and broke a bone, but even this kind of mental assurance did not allay his fear. He simply could not get around his feeling that the killer had murdered Charley and all of his reasoning did nothing to change that feeling.

He stepped into the saloon, saw that it was empty, then went inot the store. It was empty, too. He yelled, 'Charley, where the hell are you?'

Still no answer. Dan walked on past the cubby-hole in the back corner that was the post office, and called again, 'Charley.'

This time he heard the old man's quavery answer, 'Here, I'm in bed.'

Dan ran into the storeroom and turned right into the old man's living quarters, a tiny apartment that Charley had built in one corner of the cavernous warehouse where he stored what was usually a year's supply of staples, hardware, and liquor.

In this one crowded room he had a kitchen range, a table, two chairs, a bed, and a bureau. Dan found him lying in bed. His face showed no signs of a beating, so for a moment Dan

133

thought his suspicions were unfounded.

'You sick?' Dan asked.

'Yeah, I'm sick,' Charley said angrily, 'and I can tell you why. I got a hell of a beating from a big bastard that stopped here this morning for a drink. I had all I could do to get to bed. Crawled all the way from the saloon.'

Dan took a long breath, and again the prickle ran down his spine. For the first time he had some notion of what the man was like who had come to kill him. He was not just a paid assassin. He couldn't even be called a man. He was some kind of monster who hurt people for the sheer joy of hurting them.

CHAPTER EIGHTEEN

Kurt Sparks turned toward the river shortly after passing Dan Matson's ranch, dismounted, and tied his horse. He was screened by a thick wall of willows so he was not likely to be seen by anyone riding past. Actually he considered this an unnecessary precaution because it was improbable that anyone would ride past with the men cutting wood on Lone Rock and the women preparing supper.

He built a small fire on a sand bar and cooked a meal, then kicked the fire out, and rode through the willows to the trail that led north to Willets' and Carter's spreads. There had been little travel this far from the settlement. The cedars had been cut back so a wagon could get through, but Sparks did not see any trace of wagon tracks.

Obviously the two men had few if any visitors, and it was equally obvious that they didn't spend their time riding back and forth to Bald Rock. Unless someone was close enough to hear the shots, their bodies would not be discovered for days.

Sparks considered giving up the hard ride to Baggs which had no purpose except to establish an alibi and that seemed unnecessary in this situation. He would probably be perfectly safe staying in the Hole long enough to finish off Dan Matson.

On the other hand, there was a chance that Matson and the Bailey women would hear the shots if they happened to be outside and the wind was right. No, he had arranged for the relay of horses and for Orly Hunt to be in Baggs when he got there. He had always been a careful man, and there was no sense in being less careful now. Besides, there was the chance that Albright might not order Matson's killing.

He climbed two steep ridges and dropped down their north slopes, then found himself in a small valley that held two groups of ranch buildings and corrals. He counted ten horses on the hill to the east, but they were the only living things he saw as he rode up to the first cabin and dismounted. No cows, no chickens, no dogs. No sign of a garden, either. Typical bachelor quarters, he thought, a judgment which was confirmed when he stepped inside the cabin.

The place was a boar's nest, filthy and stinking, with dirty dishes piled on a table near the stove, and equally dirty blankets on the bunk. He went outside into the hot afternoon sunshine and took a deep breath. He mounted and rode on up the trail to the second cabin, which was about one hundred yards away.

He had no way of knowing which man lived in which place, but it made little difference. They were almost identical. A small stream of clear water ran down the valley. He lay on his belly and drank. It was the one good thing he could see about this location. The water was cool and sweet and held no taste of alkali.

He looked briefly into the second cabin which was cleaner than the other, but not in Sparks' opinion a decent place to live. He had always been a stickler for cleanliness, and he had never understood how human beings could live this way, then he reminded himself that they were on the dodge. Any place was better than the Texas pen, he thought. Even so, there was no excuse for a human habitation to be as filthy as these cabins were.

He rode back down the trail to the first cabin, thinking there was little chance that Willets or Carter would notice his horse's tracks. Apparently there had been no rain for a long time and the packed dirt of the trail did not hold any trace of tracks. Even if it did, the men who lived here would be unlikely to notice that the tracks were not made by one of their horses.

When he reached the lower cabin, he glanced at the corrals, noting that no horses were held there. He studied both slopes until he found what he wanted on the west slope, a boulder large enough to hide him but close enough to the cabin for accurate shooting. Also, directly above the boulder was a thicket of cedars where he could leave his horse.

He rode south along the trail, climbing steadily until he found a stretch of hard pan that lay between him and the cedar thicket. His horse would leave no tracks here as he turned off the trail, so Willets and Carter would not notice that a rider had left the trail when they rode in from their woodcutting.

Sparks rode slowly as he steadily angled up slope toward the cedars. Reaching them, he dismounted, loosened the cinch, and tied the animal, and then, jerking his Winchester from the boot, moved down the hill to the boulder.

He rested the barrel of the rifle on the boulder and found the corral gate in his sights. He would take them both as soon as they arrived if they got here while it was still daylight. If not, he would go on down to the corral and wait there in the shadows until they showed up.

For a time he let his mind dwell on the killings, but he was not a man to take his full taste of pleasure before the actual event. He leaned his rifle against the boulder, then lay on his back behind the big rock, his hat over his eyes. He dropped off to sleep at once, not waking until he heard the thud of hoofs on the trail.

He saw with alarm that the sun was down and the light was thinning rapidly. A moment later he realized with increasing alarm that they had reined up while they were still some distance from the corral gate below him. He had intended to wait until they reached the gate before he fired. It was too late to work his way down the slope to be close enough for accurate shooting, and if they didn't get a move on, it would be too dark to shoot from here.

Sparks cursed softly as he eased back the hammer of his Winchester. The two men were arguing about something, and the longer they argued the louder their voices were until finally he could make out the black man's words, 'You can do what you please, but I'm going on, Nate. I aim to sleep in my own bed tonight.'

The white man yelled back, 'Go on, then, damn it, but if I go on down with you, and that bastard is hanging around here, he'll get both of us.'

'Aw, he ain't here,' Carter shot back. 'Lee Jackson wouldn't give us the time of day, let alone warn us about a dry gulcher. He was lying if he told the schoolteacher what she claimed he did. Chances are he was trying to scare us out of the country and I sure ain't going.'

Carter didn't wait to continue the argument, but cracked steel to his horse and came on down the trail on the run, Willets hesitating, and then following slowly. Sparks was sure he could get Carter, but he might miss Willets. He made a quick decision to try. This could be the best chance he'd ever get.

He waited until Carter was directly below him, then he squeezed off a shot that knocked the black man out of his saddle. Willets wheeled his horse and started back up the trail, digging frantically with his spurs. Sparks turned his rifle on the man and began firing. The first shot was a complete miss, the second was a hit, slamming Willets forward over the horn, the third spilled him to the ground, the frightened horse pounding on up the trail.

Sparks took a long breath and straightened. The shots had sounded inordinately loud. Now there was only silence, the echoes gone. The sweet ecstasy of the kill possessed him. He stood motionless for a full minute, squeezing every bit of enjoyment he could from this moment. No other experience in his life was quite like this, nothing as fulfilling as the act of taking human life, which for a short time made him God.

Then the exalted moment was gone and the instinct of self-preservation drove him down the slope to make sure that he had done what he was being paid for and then to get out. He had never been caught at the scene of a killing, but there was always the chance that someone might be close enough to hear the shots and come nosing around.

Neither man had moved from the time they had been spilled to the ground. He made a check of Lige Carter's body, noting with satisfaction that his slug had sliced through the side of the black man's head as precisely as if he had marked an X above his ear and then had hit his target perfectly.

Quickly Sparks searched the man's pockets and took the few dollars that were in them, then ran up the trail to where Willets lay. He could have used Carter's revolver and watch, but again caution stopped him from taking them. A gun and watch could be identified.

He reached Willets' body sprawled a few feet from the trail. The second shot had caught his left shoulder, the third was perfectly placed between his shoulder blades. He took Willets' money, then wheeled and ran up the slope to the cedar thicket that held his horse.

He tightened the cinch, untied the animal, and then stood motionless for a time to listen. He heard nothing that wasn't normal, the wilderness silence complete except for the raucous call of some night bird farther up the side of the hill He mounted and rode south, angling so that he hit the trail in less than a quarter of a mile.

Once he glanced down to the valley floor, but by now the light was so thin that he could barely make out the bodies. It had worked out exactly right. If he had missed Willets, or only wounded him, he might have had a hard time getting another crack at the man.

On the other hand, if he had waited, he might never have caught them together again, and that would have made his job harder and more dangerous. He had made a snap decision, but it had been the right one, and he had found over the years that such decisions were sounder than the ones he reached by careful reasoning.

He kept on the trail, traveling fast until he reached the Matson place when he pulled his horse down to a walk. It was full dark now, and he doubted that Matson could see him if he was home, which he probably was not because no light showed in the window of his cabin.

The Bailey women were home, or at least one of them was, so he continued to hold his horse down until he was well past the ranch buildings, then cracked steel to him and started what he hoped would be a record ride to Baggs, a record so incredible that no one would believe he could have made it.

It was not until he reached the schoolhouse and saw the light in Margo Lane's window that he remembered hearing Lige Carter say that Lee Jackson had warned the teacher about his coming. Dan Matson, too, must have been warned, and that might make him hard to find.

Well, it was his good luck that Carter had not believed the warning. Willets must at least have doubted it or he wouldn't have followed Carter on down the trail. As for Jackson, he would deal with him later or let Justin Albright do it himself if he showed up in camp.

Sparks smiled at the thought as the walls of Maroon canyon closed in around him. He'd had the feeling that Albright had little trust in his ramrod. Now that his suspicion had been confirmed, he might like to rub him out personally.

CHAPTER NINETEEN

Dan Matson sat staring at Charley Klein, finding it hard to fully comprehend what the old man had said about the dry gulcher. Finally he asked, 'What did he look like?'

'He was big,' Klein answered. 'That's mostly what I remember about him. Big and mean. He was dark. Must be some kind of breed. Had a long nose. Hell, Dan, I didn't paint his picture while he was here.'

142

'That's good enough,' Dan said.

There could be no doubt about the man's identity. What Klein had just said tallied with Margo's description of the dry gulcher. Now he wished he had told Willets and Carter about the man.

'Which way did he ride?' Dan asked.

'North, I think, though I wasn't watching when he pulled out,' Klein said. 'Claimed he wanted to see Carter and Willets about buying some horses. I kept telling him he was wasting his time, but he wouldn't listen. Said he had a horse ranch in Wyoming and he was down here buying more horses. Said he was holding a herd at a ranch on Fortification creek, but I dunno, Dan. I don't think he was really after horses.'

'You're dead right about that,' Dan said. 'He's a dry gulcher that Albright hired to murder me and Willets and Carter.'

'The hell!' Klein started to sit up and fell back with a groan. 'Damn, I hurt.' He gritted his teeth until the pain passed, then he asked, 'You gonna go after him?'

'I'll wait till morning,' Dan said, 'but he's going to be hard to find.'

'Better get everybody together and comb the Hole,' Klein advised. 'It ain't so big that he can hide out very long. Chances are he's up there in the north end somewhere.'

Dan shook his head. 'It would mean that some of the others would get killed. No,

143

Charley, this is my problem, mine and Lige and Nate's. I'll go see them before they leave the schoolhouse.' He rose. 'What made him go after you?'

'I was a smart alec,' Klein admitted. 'I got sore the way he just wouldn't listen to anything I said about him wasting his time trying to see Willets and Carter. He told me I wasn't real smart, so I said he had nothing but pig slop between his ears. Well, sir, he just walked up to the bar, and before I could do anything, he grabbed me by the shoulders and hauled me across them pine boards and boogered me up all the way down to my knees. Then he shook me till I thought I was coming apart and threw me down.'

Klein took a long breath. 'After that, by God, he kicked me. Damn him, Dan, but he's big and strong.'

'You're gonna have to stay here in bed for a while,' Dan said. 'I'll ask Margo to look in on you.'

'I'd appreciate it,' Klein said. 'I might die right here where I'm lying. I'm old enough to die and I'm ready to die, but I'd sure hate to have somebody find me a month after I'm gone.'

'Can I fetch you something to eat?' Dan asked. 'Lots of grub left over.'

'Hell, no,' Klein said. 'I can't eat nothing. My belly's so sore I can't even touch it. I guess he busted up my ribs when he kicked me.'

144

'I'm sorry it happened,' Dan said. 'We'll keep an eye on you.'

He left the store, thinking that the old man was right. He might very well die right there in bed, and that would make another score to settle with Justin Albright. Sure, Dan could get the man who had ridden into the Hole to commit murder, but murder was his business.

In the end it went back to Justin Albright, and even if Dan was lucky enough to find and kill the dry gulcher, it would be like trimming the branches of a tree when the only solution was to dig out the roots. Albright could always hire another killer.

He mounted and reached the schoolhouse just as Margo was starting to the teacherage, her hands filled with dishes. He reined in beside her.

'This fellow Jackson told you about gave Charley a bad beating,' Dan said. 'He's in bed and likely to stay there a while. I told him you'd look in on him '

She nodded. 'Of course.' She looked up at Dan, her eyes troubled. 'I guess you know now I wasn't lying to you just to get you to go away with me.'

'I sure do,' Dan said, 'and I reckon you've got an apology coming.'

'You still won't leave the country?'

He shook his head. 'I can't, Margo. Damn it, you know I can't.'

'But to stay here just to get shot . . .' She

stopped, then went on, 'Dan, I thought you loved me, but you don't. If you did, you would go with me, so I'm going to marry Lee Jackson. He's asked me. I can't go on living this way any longer.'

It was crazy reasoning, he thought, for her to say he would leave the Hole with her if he loved her. She had a way of making him feel guilty because he was going back on what she considered a promise. He deserved anything she said to him, but still he felt relieved. He had known all the time that he had too many doubts about their relationship, just as he knew she was the one who had done the pushing.

'I hope you'll be happy,' he said. 'Get Jackson away from Albright and he'll be a good man.'

'He'll quit his job,' she said. 'I'll make him.'

He turned his horse and rode back to the schoolhouse, where the women were packing up and the men were drifting across the yard toward their horses. Dan looked for Willets and Carter, but did not see them. Dismounting, he asked Laura Bailey where the two men were.

'They went home,' she said. 'Bess can tell you. She was talking to them.'

Bess was coming toward them leading her horse. She motioned to Dan, calling, 'Wait. I want to ride back with you.'

He hesitated, not wanting her to ride with

146

him because the dry gulcher might be waiting for him along the road between here and his place. Besides, he knew he should be trying to catch up with Willets and Carter. But he waited, thinking she might have something to tell him.

When she reached him, she said, 'I don't know if I did the right thing or not, but I took it on myself to tell Lige and Nate about the dry gulcher. They were getting ready to pull out and I thought they ought to know.'

'I'm glad you did,' he said. 'I was figuring on riding after them.'

'You'd have trouble catching them,' she said. 'They left quite a while ago. Just after you went to the store. If you're going now, I'll ride along.'

'I'm going now,' he said, 'but I wish you'd stay here and come with your ma.'

'You don't want me riding with you?' she demanded. 'I don't intend to run after you like a certain woman does, but I wanted to go . . .'

'It's not that I don't want you riding with me,' he said. 'It's just that I'm not safe to ride with.'

'Well then,' she said, 'come on. It's been pretty dull around here lately.'

'I guess if you're looking for trouble, you'd better come.'

She tried to smile, but could not. She said lightly, 'Oh, I'm always looking for trouble.' She mounted, calling, 'Ma, I'm riding back with Dan.'

Laura Bailey nodded and waved. She knew, too, Dan thought, judging from the troubled expression on her face. He guessed the news had spread. A strange and brittle silence lay over the group. No talking, no laughter, no horseplay among the men.

He turned into the road, Bess reining in beside him, then he heard Buffalo Jack Roman call, 'Dan.' Dan stopped as Roman ran toward him.

When the rancher reached Dan, he said, 'We were just talking about this killing son that's in the Hole. I don't like it worth a damn. Maybe we oughtta stay together tonight, or get together in the morning and start looking for him.'

Dan shook his head. 'No. Me 'n' Lige and Nate will do the looking. The rest of you wait to fight Albright when the time comes.'

Roman seemed relieved. 'All right, if that's the way you want it, but if you need help, let us know.'

Dan nodded and touched up his horse, asking himself as he had so many times what would happen if he and Carter and Willets were dead. It was a good guess, and he always ended up with the same conclusion, that there would be no resistance when the Skull herd came pouring down Maroon canyon, and that, of course, was exactly what Albright thought.

Bess didn't say a word until they reached

the Bailey place. Dan glanced at her several times, not knowing what to make of her expression. He had never seen her really worried before, but she was now.

Usually she had a quick, smart remark to make, often an insulting one, and she would follow with a hearty laugh, but this evening she was gravely silent. Once he thought he actually saw tears in her eyes, but he must have imagined that. Bess Bailey was not one to cry about anything.

When they reached her house, she stepped down. Dan said, 'I'll probably see you tomorrow.'

She said, 'Get down, Dan. Please.'

He hesitated, wanting to go on. Just being here with her might be dangerous for her. He glanced uneasily toward the river and its screen of willows, then brought his gaze back to her.

'I don't like standing here with you,' he said as he dismounted. 'If he cuts loose at me, he might decide to shoot anybody who's with me.'

'I want you to stay here tonight, Dan,' she whispered. 'It's hard for me to beg, but please do it. I'm ... I'm scared.'

He looked at her, not knowing what to make of this. She wasn't the tough, masculine Bess Bailey he had known ever since her father had died. At this moment she was very feminine and vulnerable and, he decided, truly frightened.

'You've got nothing to be scared about if I ain't here,' he said. 'I don't think Laura would want me hanging around till we catch that bastard.'

She had let her reins drop. She said softly, 'It ain't Ma who loves you, Dan. It's me and I don't want you killed.'

She threw her arms around him and hugged. With her mouth pressed against his chest, she said, her voice muffled, 'I couldn't live if he killed you. I just couldn't, Dan.'

CHAPTER TWENTY

For Dan Matson this had been a strange day. It had started that way with Margo Lane telling him about the dry gulcher; it was ending on even a stranger note, with Bess hugging him and saying she couldn't live if the dry gulcher killed him

It made no sense at all to Dan. He could not keep from saying, 'I don't get it, Bess. You've been fighting with me ever since your pa died. I figured you didn't give a damn about whether I lived or died.'

She jerked back. 'Oh, you didn't? Well, why did you think I was fighting with you? You're a stupid man, Dan Matson. We used to ride to school together and you used to take me to dances and parties and you even kissed me a

150

few times, but you kept on the same way after Pa died and I needed you so much. You acted like I was a . . . a sister or maybe a cousin.'

She whirled away from him, choked, then cried out, 'My God, Dan, you must have known I loved you. I wanted you and you were right here under my nose but as far away as the moon.' She stopped and swallowed, and finally added, 'And all the time that damned floozy of a schoolteacher was flipping her hips at you every time you looked in her direction. I could have killed her.'

He grabbed her by the shoulders and turned her around so that she faced him. He said hotly, 'Sure I'm stupid. Any man's stupid when it comes to figuring out a woman. All I knew was that you changed and tried being a man.'

'We had to have a man after Pa died,' she flared. 'We couldn't afford to hire one. Somebody had to do the work.' She wiped her eyes and ran a sleeve across her nose. 'You just took me for granted like a rock up there on the rim. I thought that if I acted different . . . like not being a lady . . . you'd notice me.'

'Oh, I noticed you, all right,' he shouted angrily. 'By God, I noticed you from the day you put pants on. If you think that's any way to attract a man, you've been eating a hell of a lot of loco weed.'

They stood three feet apart, glaring at each other, his hands gripping her arms so hard he bruised her. Then suddenly she laughed shakily. 'I guess I'm as bad as Margo the way she's been running after you. I said I'd never do that, Dan, but I wanted to. I've been so mad at her . . .'

'Forget Margo,' he said. 'She's going to marry Lee Jackson. She told me this evening.'

Then he did something he had never thought he would do. He put his arms around her and brought her to him and kissed her, hard and thoroughly. He had kissed her before a few times, but never like this.

When he finally released his grip on her, she did not pull back, but kept her arms on his shoulders, her lips very close to his. She said softly, 'Dan, do I have to run after you anymore?'

'No, you've caught me,' he said. 'I'll take care of the horses. You go into the house and put on a dress.'

She nodded and turned from him, then stopped. 'Dan, you will stay here tonight?'

'Sure, if that's what you want,' he said. 'And another thing. As soon as we get this ruckus settled, you're going to marry me.'

'Send for the preacher now,' she urged. 'Why do we have to wait till the fight's over?'

'I don't know who to send,' he said. 'I can't leave the Hole.'

'Send the Sanders boy,' she said. 'He's old enough to make the ride.'

'I guess I could,' he said. 'He's a good rider and I don't think Albright's men would bother a boy.'

She turned toward the house again, and this time did not stop or turn back. He watered the horses and stripped gear from them, all the time remembering how often he had told himself that he was sure of one thing. Bess Bailey did not love him. Well, he guessed he didn't know what went on in a woman's mind or heart.

He saw Laura Bailey coming in her buggy and waited for her by the corral gate. When she stopped, he gave her a hand down. He said, 'Laura, you'd better get ready for a shock. Bess is in the house putting on a dress. We're going to get married.'

She smiled, nodded, and tried to look surprised, but it was plain she wasn't shocked. 'Congratulations! I don't know how you managed it, her being so stubborn.'

'I didn't manage it,' he admitted. 'She did. She said I was stupid. I guess I was.'

Laura laughed. 'Oh, I think she was the stupid one. I kept telling her she was playing her game too long and hard, but she wouldn't listen. I don't know how many times she cried herself to sleep over you, but she wouldn't change. You'll have to put up with her stubborn streak, so I hope you can be patient with her. She's a good girl, Dan, and she loves you.'

Laura shook her head. 'But she's headstrong. That's a side of her you've never understood. Her pa spoiled her. He never understood, either, but between you 'n' me, there's been times when she's hard to live with. You'll hit some times like that, too.'

'I reckon so,' he admitted, 'but then maybe I'm a little mule-headed, too.'

'Indeed, you are.' Laura nodded agreement. 'Like leaving the country till this blows over. That's what we think you ought to do just to stay alive, but I wouldn't ask you because I know you wouldn't do it.'

'Maybe it's the stupid part of me that says I'm staying,' he said. 'Anyhow, you're right, so don't ask me. Go on in. I'll take care of your horse.'

He took his time, hoping he would never see Bess in man's clothes again, but he knew he would because there would be times when the work required more than one man and he would need her help.

Still, knowing that she would be wearing a dress, he was not really prepared for what he saw when he went into the house. He heard the fire popping when he stepped through the front door; he smelled coffee and frying ham, and heard her call, 'I'm back here, Dan.'

He crossed the front room and then stopped, sucking his breath in audibly. She stood by the range, but she made a half turn so he could see her face. She was smiling at him, wanting him to know that she was a very happy woman.

154

Her hair hung down her back in a glossy, black mass. She was wearing a freshly starched dress, pink and white checked, with a tight-fitting bodice. He had never been fully aware before of her taut, trim breasts as long as he had known her. She'd tied a red apron around her waist, the color startlingly bright because it contrasted so sharply with the white border.

'Come in and you can pour yourself a cup of coffee,' Bess said.

He walked toward her slowly, shaking his head. 'Where have you been, Bess Bailey?' he asked.

Her smile faded. 'Hiding in a man's blue shirt and Levis,' she said, 'but I'm not hiding any longer. I'm out in the open.'

He kissed her, a kiss so long that Laura said from the living room door, 'I hate to interrupt anything as important as this, but I'm hungry and you're going to burn that ham if you don't start paying some attention to it. You two can live on love, but I can't.'

Bess pushed him away. 'We're going to stay at your place, Dan. I refuse to live in the same house with my mother who tells me how long I can kiss you.'

Laura sniffed. 'That's the best news I've heard for a long time. Now I'll be free to do what I want to in my own house. I've always heard that it never worked to put two women under one roof.'

'Two women?' Bess turned the ham in the

frying pan, then added, 'This is the first time you've had another woman under this roof for a long time.'

'Not so,' Laura said as she started setting the table. 'She's been playacting, so don't let her fool you, Dan. She's been a woman every evening after the supper dishes were put away. She'd knit or make a dress or embroider. Why, I've seen her stand in front of her . . .'

'Ma!'

Bess turned from the range, her face red, her lips tightly pressed. Laura laughed. 'Dan, when she calls me Ma and uses that tone of voice, I know it's time to retreat.'

Dan poured a cup of coffee and took it to the table and sat down. He said, 'You know, Laura, I'm marrying a strange woman.'

'I am a very strange woman, Mr. Matson,' Bess said. 'If I can keep you alive, I aim to make your life exciting from now on.'

'You will,' he said. 'You certainly will.'

CHAPTER TWENTY-ONE

Dan slept in the barn that night. Or tried to. He would doze off, then wake up, every sense alert, right hand gripping the butt of his gun. He would listen for a moment, then shut his eyes and try to relax, but he found sleep elusive.

156

Bess had told him that the dog would raise the roof if anyone came snooping around within fifty yards of the place, but still Dan could not get out of his mind the possibility that the dry gulcher might be outside the barn or across the road waiting for him to make an appearance.

He knew he was jumping at shadows. If the killer was after him, he'd be watching Dan's house, not the Bailey place, but this self-assurance did little to relieve the tension that he felt. Also, he was worried about Carter and Willets, thinking he should have ridden to their ranches before dark. Morning might be too late.

He finally dropped off to sleep, only to be awakened by a noisy rooster who wasn't satisfied to announce the new day once, but kept on crowing until Dan gave up. He stepped outside. It was not yet full light. For a time he stood with his back to the barn wall studying the shadows, but he did not see or hear anything suspicious.

Deciding he was being overly cautious, he strode across the yard to the log trough and washed his face, his ears attuned for any sound that wasn't normal. Prickles chased each other up and down his spine as he wondered if he would hear the shot that would kill him, or would he feel the brutal impact of the bullet and then hear the shot? Still he heard nothing except the continued crowing of the eager rooster.

Smoke was pouring from the chimney. He went into the house to find Laura cooking breakfast. A moment later Bess came out of her bedroom. She was wearing a different dress than the one she had worn the previous evening, a bright blue dress that was cut to show off her figure as favorably as the checked dress.

Dan was surprised to see that she had a very attractive figure and thought how completely he had failed to notice it during the months he had seen her only in men's clothes. He asked, 'How many dresses do you have?'

'Dozens,' she said, smiling.

She came to him and kissed him, and for a time he held her in his arms, still finding it hard to realize the change in her and in their relationship. For a time Laura ignored them, then she said tartly, 'Bess, quit your lallygagging and help me. I never thought I'd live to see the day when this would go on in my kitchen. I tell you, Dan, Bess's father and me never carried on like this.'

Bess snorted derisively. 'You're lying and you know it. I remember even when I was a little girl how you and Pa behaved. It was a scandal. That's what it was. A scandal!'

Laura laughed delightedly. 'See how she is, Dan? She calls her own mother a liar.'

'You can see how it is, too,' Bess said as she carried dishes to the table. 'She's still trying to run my life. I guess I won't wait till we're married. I'll move in with you today.'

'No you won't,' Dan said. 'It would be bad enough to make you a widow after we're married, but I sure ain't going to do it before.'

Bess glanced at him, a worried frown creasing her forehead. 'What are we going to do today?'

'I don't know what you're going to do,' Dan said, 'but I'm going to go see Willets and Carter. I should have gone last night. I don't figure this dry gulcher will wait.'

'I'll go, too,' Bess said. 'I'll have to take my dress off. I don't aim to start riding side saddle just because you like me in a dress better than in pants.'

'I hoped you'd never wear pants again,' Dan said.

'You knew better,' she snapped. 'There's a time for pants and a time for a dress.'

'That reminds me,' Laura said. 'I've got a question to ask. Am I losing my cowhand? How are you going to handle two spreads, Dan?'

'We can work 'em together,' he answered. 'You can go on growing a garden and raising chickens and pigs. We'll help you eat your garden sass and eggs and pork.'

Laura threw up her hands. 'I don't know about this love business. Seems to me I'm the loser.'

'You'll get me out of your house,' Bess said.

'That ought to be worth something.'

Laura gave her a quick glance, then turned away to hide the tears that were in her eyes. 'It will be a mixed blessing,' she said in a low tone. 'Sit down, Dan. It's ready.'

Dan took a chair at the table, thinking that he would not have the mother-in-law problem that so many men had. Laura Bailey was an unusual woman in a good many ways.

Dan rose as soon as he finished eating. He said, 'Bess, I wish you'd stay here. This might turn out to be a little risky.'

'It'll be damned risky and you know it,' she snapped. 'That's why I'm going with you.'

He hesitated, wanting to tell her she couldn't go, but he didn't want to quarrel with her and destroy the good feeling that had replaced the old hostility.

'I don't want to put you in a position where you'll be a target,' he said. 'I'd just feel better if I knew you were safe here in the house.'

She sensed his feeling and rose, saying simply, 'Dan, I've loved you for so long, and most of that time we were both acting like a couple of brats. If you're going to get shot at, I want to be there. If I stayed here, I'd be worrying every minute till I saw you coming back down the road.'

He understood how she felt, and he also knew that he could not make her stay here, that there would be times like this after they were married when he would have to let her have her way. As her mother had said, she was a headstrong girl, and so, against his better judgment, he said, 'If you're bound to go, I'll saddle your horse.'

A few minutes later they rode north past his place and on toward the first ridge that lay between his spread and Willets' and Carter's ranches. His uneasiness increased until it seemed unbearable, his gaze constantly searching the willows for any hint of the dry gulcher's presence, and then turning toward the rim to the east.

They topped the ridge and rode down the north side, Dan's nervousness diminishing now that they were away from the river with its thick screen of willows. It seemed unlikely that the killer would be hiding here. There was no cover on either side, except for an occasional juniper or boulder that dotted the slope.

The dry gulcher, of course, would have no way of knowing that one of his victims would be riding along here at this early morning hour. Again he was reassured by thinking that if the man was still around, he would have been back somewhere in the willows near the buildings waiting for him to show himself. By now, of course, he would have made his try as Dan and Bess had ridden by. Since he hadn't, Dan could accept the fact that he was gone.

This line of reasoning brought him to the certainty that the gunman had left the country. If he had succeeded in killing Carter and

Willets, there was a good possibility that he had gone somewhere else to establish an alibi. He certainly knew he had been seen when he'd ridden past the schoolhouse; he had left Charley Klein alive, so he knew the old man could identify him.

The chances were, then, that he had returned to the Skull camp with the idea that the men there would swear he had left the Hole early in the afternoon shortly after he had been in Klein's saloon and therefore could not have committed the murders because both Carter and Willets had been cutting wood at that time.

Dan could not avoid what seemed a fact that both Willets and Carter were dead, or perhaps the fear was so strong in him that he believed it was true, but fearing it and knowing it were two very different things.

When he topped the second ridge and saw Willets' body beside the trail below them and Carter sprawled on the ground down near the corral gate, he reined up and sat his saddle, unable for a moment to breathe. When his heart finally stopped hammering so violently and he was able to draw a full breath, he thought he was going to be sick.

'My God,' Bess said hoarsely. 'I didn't really think we'd find them this way. The bastard's been here and gone.'

'I'm going to have a look around,' Dan said, 'then I'll hook Carter's team to his wagon and take the bodies to Charley's saloon. I want you to ride back and tell everybody what's happened. Tell 'em to be at the saloon before dark. We'll decide what to do.'

He expected her to argue, but she did not. She turned her horse and rode back the way they had come. He was sorry she had seen the bodies, he thought, but maybe it was better this way. She would not have to see them again when they were laid out in the saloon.

CHAPTER TWENTY-TWO

Kurt Sparks arrived in Baggs late at night after having made the ride from Smith's Hole in a time that would not be believed by anyone. The sad part of it was, he thought, that the only person he could brag to was Orly Hunt.

He left his horse in the hands of a sleepy-eyed hostler in a livery stable and went directly to the hotel, noting that the bar was the only saloon that was still open. He signed the register, took the key to his room from the night clerk, and stepped into the bar.

Orly Hunt sat in the rear of the room, his feet on a table, his hat canted to the back of his head. The bartender was telling him to go to bed, that he had kept the place open longer than usual and he was closing up.

Hunt rose and said he guessed it was time

163

and left the bar. Sparks asked for a drink as he tossed a coin onto the cherrywood surface. He yawned and stretched, then he said, 'I've been up north looking for horses, but I didn't find any I wanted. I might as well have stayed home.'

The bartender poured his drink, saying, 'You're the gent who was in here the other day asking about horses. I told you then I didn't figure you'd find any except maybe in Smith's Hole.'

'I was there,' Sparks said, 'but I didn't see any animals I'd buy for what they were asking, so I left about noon and swung north like I said. Hell, I've been riding most of the day and damned near all night.' He shook his head. 'No, this just ain't horse country. I'll take a *pasear* along Bear river tomorrow, but I've about given up.'

'Finish your drink,' the bartender said. 'I'm going to bed. That damned Orly Hunt kept me up longer 'n I like to stay. Kept telling me his adventures. I've knowed him for years and I never knew he was the tough hand he claims to be. You know, he sat right over there and swore he was the one who shot Jesse James.'

Sparks laughed. 'You run into all kinds, I guess. He sure must be some liar.'

'He was for a fact,' the bartender said. 'I felt like laughing in his face, but that would have made him mad.'

Sparks finished his drink and set the glass

down. 'I'm riding south in the morning so I probably won't see you again unless I come back this way.'

The bartender shook his head. 'Probably not. I'm sleeping till noon. Well, good luck. I hope you find your horses.'

Sparks nodded. 'Thanks.'

He went upstairs to his room and was pulling off his boots when he heard a knock on his door. He called, 'Come in.'

Orly Hunt slipped into the room after glancing along the hall. He asked, 'Finish your job?'

'Two,' Sparks said. 'That's all I contracted for.'

Hunt handed him an envelope. 'It's there. Every cent Albright promised to pay. He rode into camp just after you left. He's fixing to stay till after we get the herd into the Hole. He's sore because the Hole ranchers haven't sold out to him before now. He's so used to having his own way that he don't savvy why folks don't jump every time he hollers.'

'They ain't ordinary homesteaders down there,' Sparks said. 'I figure they'll fight.'

Hunt nodded. 'So do I, but Albright never listens to nobody. He was damned sore because you showed your face in camp. He didn't want nobody knowing you had anything to do with us. Now the Skull riders know. Some of 'em might talk.'

Sparks shook his head. 'Nobody remembers

me. It don't pay for anybody to remember me unless I want 'em to, like I want the bartender downstairs to remember me. Better pass the word.'

'I will,' Hunt said worriedly, 'though I guess nobody gives a damn except Lee Jackson. I don't know what to do about him. I've been telling him it's too late to change sides, that he should have pulled out several days ago if he's going to. He says he won't take the herd into the Hole, but hell, that's the reason Albright's kept him on. I figure Albright will fire him as soon as we finish what we're starting, but he says he'll hang on till we're ready to go down Maroon canyon, which same don't make no sense.'

'He's a God-damned nothing,' Sparks said angrily. 'I spotted him the minute I seen him. I'm surprised that Albright kept him this long.'

'He's a good ramrod,' Hunt said.

'I don't believe it,' Sparks snapped. 'You tell Albright he's kept Jackson too long already. He told the Hole bunch that Albright had hired an exterminator. It's lucky I got Willets and Carter, and the only reason I did was that they thought Jackson was lying. Now what about Matson?'

'That's your next job,' Hunt answered, 'and get it done pronto.'

'It ain't gonna be easy now,' Sparks said. 'They'll be watching for me. He should have told me for sure. I could have got Matson before I left the Hole.'

He had thought about it all the way to Baggs, and he'd made up his mind that he'd have to get Matson from the rim, that to ride down into the Hole again would be suicide.

'I reckon he should have,' Hunt agreed as he stood up and yawned. 'I'd better go to . . .'

'You're paying for Matson tonight,' Sparks said. 'I ain't hanging around this country once I get that yahoo. I figure I've got myself clear on the Carter and Willets job with the bartender seeing me and knowing when I got here, but I'd be in a hornet's nest if I went back.'

Hunt shook his head. 'I can't pay you now and you know it. You get paid after you do the job.'

Sparks shrugged. 'It's up to you. Most of the time I deal that way, but when I do, I've got to be in position to get my pay. This time I won't be. The minute I plug Matson, I'm riding north. I've got some work lined out in Wyoming, and I aim to live long enough to do it.'

'I tell you I can't do it,' Hunt said, raising his voice. 'Albright would skin me and hang my hide up to dry if I paid you and you didn't get the job done.'

Sparks started to unbutton his shirt. 'Then go after Matson yourself. Now get to hell out of here. I'm aiming to sleep three hours and then light out. In a day or two I'll find me a quiet spot in Wyoming and sleep for a week.'

Horn stood staring at him, then swore angrily as he took his wallet from his pocket and counted out five $100 greenbacks. 'By God, you're a dead man if you don't earn this money. Albright will put the hounds on your trail till they get you.'

'I always earn my money,' Sparks said complacently as he put the greenbacks into his money belt. 'I hear you shot Jesse James.'

'I got Frank, too,' Hunt snapped, and walked out of the room.

Sparks laughed silently as he pulled off his pants and lay down. He'd get Matson sooner or later. What he hadn't told Hunt was that it might be later. The man would be jumpy if he had found out about Carter and Willets and be hard to kill If he didn't know, Sparks might get him from the rim tonight, and then he would head north. He wasn't familiar with the country, but he knew he'd come out somewhere around Rock Springs. He could hole up there and be safe.

He went to sleep at once. He woke shortly after sunup, dressed, and went down for breakfast. He was a man who never needed much sleep when his work was still unfinished unless it ran on for several days. This was something he had taught himself, to go without sleep until he could relax, and make it up in some whorehouse where he knew the madam and would be safe for as long as he wanted to stay.

He was on the road back to Smith's Hole within minutes after he finished breakfast. He would not have to ride so hard today. The trick was to get on the rim above Matson's place and simply wait for him to show up. He would have to see how it looked, but if he had good light and there was no wind, he was confident he could do the job from the rim.

He had been doubtful yesterday, but the more he thought about it, the more reluctant he was to go back into the Hole. He'd have to wait until after dark, and even then they might have someone guarding the lower end of Maroon canyon who would either shoot him or raise an alarm.

It was his sense of caution that forced his decision. Sometimes he made snap judgments that disregarded the cautious approach, but whenever he had time to wool something over, he felt more comfortable with carefully made decisions. He might not get Matson as soon as Albright wanted because the cowman was in a hurry, but he'd get him no matter how much time it took.

He stayed on the north side of the Little Snake, so that Albright and the Skull crew would not see him. He reached the upper end of Maroon canyon in the middle of the afternoon with thunderheads boiling up over the western rim. He rode on, keeping back from the edge so that no one in the Hole would catch a glimpse of him if the rider happened to look in his direction.

Even if the bodies had not been found, the Hole men had been warned and would be alert. He cursed Jackson, thinking how much easier his job would be if the man had not given the schoolteacher the warning.

Sparks glanced up at the tip of Lone Rock and saw the pile of trees. A signal fire, he thought. They'd wasted their time getting it ready. With Willets, Carter, and Matson gone, they probably wouldn't work together in resisting Albright. But he had told Hunt they would fight and maybe they would. He had never respected sod busters, but small ranchers like the ones in the Hole were made of a tougher fiber. He dismissed the question from his thoughts. It was Albright's and Hunt's problem, not his.

He stopped twice and eased his way to the rim until he identified the place where he could look down directly on the Matson buildings. When he finally reached the exact spot, he did not see any movement around either the Bailey or Matson ranches.

Worming away from the rim, he returned to his horse, took his glasses from a saddle bag, and snaked back to the rim. He made a study of the buildings below him, then of the Bailey place, then of Bald Rock. It was quite a ways from here, but he saw a long line of horses tied in front of the saloon. Every man in the Hole

170

must be there, he thought. Even as he watched, the men filed out of the saloon, mounted, and disappeared up Maroon canyon.

He rose and walked back to his horse, knowing that he was in for a long wait. He wasn't sure what was happening, but he could guess. The chances were that Justin Albright and the Skull crew would have an opportunity to gun Matson down before he would.

Albright would be sore as hell, but Sparks told himself that it wasn't his fault that his quarry wasn't home. He'd wait. If Albright or some of his cowhands didn't get Matson, he would come home sooner or later and Sparks would kill him when he did.

He had been so engrossed with his scheming that he was not aware of the black clouds that had covered the sky. Now a booming clap of thunder jarred him and he glanced up at the sky. He swore and quickly untied his slicker from behind the saddle and put it on. A moment later it began to rain, a few drops at first, and then it seemed as if the sky opened up and came at him in a downpour.

CHAPTER TWENTY-THREE

Justin Albright rode into camp unannounced early in the afternoon on the day Sparks killed Nate Willets and Lige Carter. Lee Jackson had not expected him to show up, so he was shocked when he saw who the visitor was. As Albright dismounted beside the wagon, Jackson said to Orly Hunt in a low voice, 'What the hell is that bastard doing here?'

'He came for the kill,' Hunt answered. 'That's his way. He figures it's about over with by now.'

Albright called a cheerful greeting to the cook, then strode toward Hunt, asking, 'Have they all come in and agreed to sell?'

For just a moment Hunt hesitated as if knowing what was going to happen, and then, seeing no way out of this dilemma, he said, 'I'm sorry, Mr. Albright. None of them have come in.'

Albright stared at Hunt as if he could not believe it. Jackson, looking at him, thought the man had arranged his timetable, and how he could not accept the fact that events had failed to keep pace with that timetable.

'Hasn't Sparks showed up yet?' Albright demanded.

Hunt nodded. 'He rode by a while ago. I reckon he's in the Hole by now.'

'You mean he stopped here?' Albright bellowed.

'Yeah,' Hunt said. 'He told me to arrange a relay of horses so he could make a fast ride to Baggs.'

'I'll kill the son of a bitch,' Albright said. 'I didn't want the crew to know he was in the county or had anything to do with us.'

Hunt shrugged. 'I wondered about that, but he's a cautious man. Maybe he wanted you tied in so you'd have to defend him if he got caught.'

'The hell I will,' Albright snapped. 'Anyhow, I told him the law in this county wouldn't touch him.' The cattleman hesitated, then asked, 'You gonna see him in Baggs?'

Hunt nodded. 'I figured to.'

'Tell him to get back to Smith's Hole and finish his job if he hasn't already,' Albright said angrily. 'He'll earn fifteen hundred dollars, not a thousand.'

'I'll tell him,' Hunt promised.

Albright wheeled to face Jackson, one arm swinging toward the cattle that had spread out to graze on the hills to the south. 'You're dilly-dallying. Get that herd moving. I ain't going to wait much longer. If those ten-cow ranchers in the Hole haven't showed up by tomorrow night to sell, we'll move into the Hole. We'll shoot any man who stands in our way and we'll burn every ranch house and barn down there.'

Jackson stared at him, hating him and

173

despising him as he had never hated or despised a man before in his life. Albright must have lost his senses. There was no hurry about moving the herd except Albright's impatience.

Common sense would dictate waiting until the murders of Willets and Carter were known to every man in Smith's Hole, and later that of Dan Matson. It was Jackson's judgment that the killing of Matson would break the will to resist, but it would also be the final act of violence that would destroy Albright because it was something the sheriff could not ignore. It was strange that Albright had not seen that.

'Give them more time, Albright,' Jackson said. 'There's women and kids down there. If you go into the Hole to shoot and burn, they'll get hurt.'

'That's their lookout,' Albright stormed. 'Now, by God, you get out there and move that herd. And don't call me Albright. I'm Mr. Albright to you.'

For a moment Jackson stood motionless, anger a rising force in him that threatened to explode into uncontrolled fury, but the old habits of compliance and indecision were still too strong. He turned away, saying nothing, and mounted and rode away.

The familiar self-accusations that had plagued him for weeks began to torture him again. He had kept saying he would leave before the Skull herd was driven into the Hole.

The truth was he had kept hoping it would never happen, but now it was going to happen in another thirty-six hours unless Albright changed his plan, and Jackson sensed that the cowman had reached the point where he could not turn back.

Jackson couldn't help Dan Matson any more than he had. He had delivered his warning, which was all that could be expected of him. If Matson stayed in the Hole to be dry gulched by Sparks, it was his affair. He had made the decision, but now Jackson had something else to worry about. Margo Lane was in Smith's Hole. Even Albright would not kill a woman by intention, but he might very well bring about her death by accident.

All afternoon Jackson waged the same mental war with himself that he had been fighting for weeks. The only difference was in degree. In the past he had found relief from the agony of making the final decision because the time had not come. Now it had come, and the fact that Margo's life would be in danger when Albright made his move added tension that pulled his nerves tight.

The cattle were edged toward the mouth of Maroon canyon that afternoon. By evening they were close enough to cross the Little Snake the following day and be ready to move down the canyon the next morning.

Hunt had left long before Jackson returned to camp that night. He exchanged no words with Albright, who looked at him with ill-concealed contempt, and he stared back at the cowman with the same contempt. He had never found the courage to do this before, but now he didn't care what Albright thought. He wasn't even sure that the cattleman was aware of his feeling or whether he gave a damn one way or the other.

Tomorrow he would ask Hunt for his wages and ride into the Hole. He would get Margo out if he could. If not, at least he would be there to defend her. Maybe he could keep the Skull men from burning the teacherage.

He knew, of course, that Margo might refuse to go with him, but he had to try. All of his planning had been so interwoven with Margo that he could not face the possibility of finally losing her.

Jackson slept very little that night. He stared at the sky, black except for the scattering of stars, and thought that the blackness fitted his mood. Tomorrow was the day he had been afraid would come, the day when he would make his break with Skull and give up a job that he had enjoyed and which had paid well. He told himself sourly it was a decision he should have made days ago. Now it was being forced upon him. Somewhere every man drew a line. He drew his before he would lead the Skull men into Smith's Hole to burn and murder the men who lived there.

The more he thought about it, the more he

loathed himself for not making this decision long ago. Basically he was a coward. He realized he had never been a man who made a decision easily. This one had been different from any he had faced before because he had been afraid to cut loose from Skull, to take the gamble that any man takes when he goes out on his own.

As soon as breakfast was over, he rode out to the herd and gave the order to drive it across the Little Snake. It took more time than he had figured on, so it was well into the afternoon when he returned to camp and found that Hunt had just ridden in.

'Sparks says he'll earn the other five hundred dollars,' Hunt was saying to Albright. 'He insisted that I pay him before he finished the last job. He said he wouldn't be around afterwards to collect, that he was heading north the minute he finished.'

'You done a fool thing,' Albright snapped. 'You know I never pay a man before he's carried out his agreement.'

'I know, I know,' Hunt snapped back. 'I had no choice. He would have ridden off without getting Matson and I figure he's the key man. You should have put him on top of the list instead of at the bottom.'

Albright didn't like being criticized, but he wheeled away from Hunt to face Jackson without making an issue out of it. 'What are you doing back here?'

177

Jackson ignored the question. He said to Hunt, 'I want my time.'

'Your time?' Albright asked as if he could not believe he had heard the request. 'Did you say you want your time?'

'That's what I said,' Jackson agreed. 'I signed on to run a cattle outfit, not to shoot honest ranchers and burn them out. I've had a bellyful, Albright.'

The cowman's face turned purple. 'By God, you'll get your time when I say so. Men don't quit on me. I fire 'em, and you're fired the minute we finish in Smith's Hole. Now get back to your job.'

'Then I'm fired right now,' Jackson said. 'Give me my money, Orly. You had it for Sparks, didn't you?'

'Yeah, but . . .'

'You ain't giving him nothing, Orly,' Albright said in the high-pitched voice of a man who had lost all control of his emotions. 'You get back out there or I'll kill you. You've given me all the trouble you're going to. I should have kept you fired instead of letting Judge Verling talk me out of it. I saw in Denver that you were a nothing, a big nothing.'

It happened, then, the thing that had threatened to happen many times. The indecision, the insecurity, the basic cowardice that had emasculated Lee Jackson for so long was swept away. Instead, he could only see

178

Albright as a maniac, a monster, and he knew he would be destroyed if he didn't quit now.

'I'd rather be a nothing than a man who has lost his senses the way you have,' Jackson said. 'You're a killer of women and babies, and by God, I don't know why I've stuck with you this long. I'm ashamed that I have. You can keep my money and go to hell with it.'

He wheeled his horse and rode away. He heard a strange gasping sound of rage and disbelief behind him, and told himself that Justin Albright had never been talked to that way before. For the first time in his life Lee Jackson was filled with pride, the warm feeling that at last he was his own man.

He heard the shot and felt the numbing impact of the slug that slammed into his back, but he wasn't knocked out of his saddle. Somehow he gripped the horn and stayed on his horse. He knew he was hit hard and that he was bleeding, and he realized that everything was distorted, all sight and all sound, but he also knew that his only chance for life was to reach Margo.

Somehow he got across the Little Snake. He came to the head of Maroon canyon and began to sway, his grip on the horn slackening, and then the blackness closed in around him and he slid to the ground. His horse trotted on down the road between the slanted red walls toward Bald Rock.

CHAPTER TWENTY-FOUR

Dan Matson carried the bodies of Lige Carter and Nate Willets into Charley Klein's saloon and laid them on the floor in the center of the room. Charley hobbled out of bed and sat down in a chair at one of the tables. He stared angrily at the bodies and shook his head.

'The son of a bitch done it,' Charley said. 'He beat hell out of me and killed two good men.'

Dan found a canvas in the back room and covered the bodies. It was then a few minutes after twelve. Bess came in, saying, 'They'll be here, but they're going to ask what you're aiming to do. Talk some more?'

'No,' Dan answered, and let it go at that.

'He ain't gonna bring 'em back to life,' Charley said, 'but he can send Lee Jackson and the rest of the Skull bunch to hell to live with 'em.'

'Not Jackson,' Dan said somberly. 'I ain't sure which side he's on or even if he knows himself, but he did bring us the warning. If we'd taken it seriously, Nate and Lige would be alive.'

'They knew,' Bess reminded him. 'They should have taken the warning seriously.'

No one said anything for a long time after that. It didn't really help, Dan thought, for anyone to say it was their own fault. He should have done something instead of coming over here and talking to Charley, which was what he had done. He felt guilty because he hadn't done anything.

Presently the Hole ranchers began drifting in. All of them did practically the same thing. They tied in front, walked into the saloon, nodded at the others who were here, then turned the canvas back, looked at the faces of the dead men, and replaced the canvas.

Charley had set a bottle on the bar. Some of the men poured themselves drinks, some sat at the tables, and others paced restlessly around the room. No one felt like talking except in monosyllables and in low, hushed tones, and no one said anything about being hungry.

Dan sensed a different atmosphere than he had in previous meetings. Before the attitude had been to wait until Skull made its move. Now Dan told himself that the time of waiting was over, the time for talking was gone, and he was convinced that every man here felt the same way.

He stood at the end of the bar watching the grim-faced men in the room and noting the lack of small talk that was characteristic of such gatherings. The truth was that after all the talk and planning and threats, no one had really come to grips with the danger that had threatened them.

Now two dead men lay on the floor, and the

depressing knowledge faced them that all or any of them might wind up the same way. It was this knowledge that created the tension, an impatience to get the trouble over with.

The pressure was greater on Dan than anyone else because he was one of the three men who had been scheduled to die. He could not live this way, his skin constantly crawling in anticipation of a bullet slamming into him from the rim above him or from some hiding place along the road. He would go after the dry gulcher himself if he had to rather than keep looking over his shoulder and jumping at every strange sound.

Buffalo Jack Roman was the last to arrive. He looked at the bodies, replaced the canvas over their faces, and straightened up, his gaze on Dan's face as he asked, 'What are we going to do? Send for the sheriff?'

Dan shook his head. 'Buck Douglas didn't like Nate and Lige very well. He'd come if we sent for him, but I don't think he'd work very hard to bring the killer in.'

'He'd give the bastard a reward,' Charley Klein muttered.

'Well then,' Roman said sourly, 'you must have had some notion in your noggin when you sent for us. You figure to bury these men this afternoon?'

'The burying will wait till tomorrow,' Dan answered. 'When I asked Bess to have you come here, I thought we'd just talk our situation over and make our move tomorrow, but I've changed my mind. We've just talked about defending ourselves. I believe that's the wrong way to go at this. We know now what Albright will do. I guess none of us really believed it even after Jackson sent us the warning. I think it's time we stopped talking about defending ourselves and go after them.'

'Well, by God,' Roman said. 'I figured we'd just do some more palavering and go home. We ain't gonna get back to work till we run that Skull herd into Wyoming.'

Dan shook his head. 'Maybe we won't get back to work then, Jack. We've got to remember that it's not the cattle or Lee Jackson or the Skull hands who are the enemy. It's Justin Albright. Running the Skull herd into Wyoming or shooting the Skull hands ain't gonna do the job for us.'

'It'll be a start,' Roman said doggedly. 'At least we'll show Albright it ain't gonna be as easy as he figured.'

The others nodded agreement, and Dan knew he had assessed their feelings correctly. He said, 'All right, we'll hit 'em today. Anybody who don't want to stomp out snakes, say so.'

Several of them said, 'We're ready.'

'Some of us will die,' Dan said. 'If you want to tell your wives goodbye . . .'

'Let's get on with it.' Roman pointed at the dead men. 'They were our friends. It ain't just what may happen to you, Dan, or any of the rest of us. It's squaring accounts with Skull. We'll scatter that herd from hell to breakfast.'

'Then let's move,' Dan said.

He started toward the door. Bess had not said a word all afternoon. Now she stepped in front of Dan, put her arms around him and kissed him. 'For once I'm not going with the men. I'll stay with Margo. You come back, Dan.' Suddenly tears were in her eyes as she whispered, 'I guess women have sent their men off to war from the beginning of time, but I never knew how it was until this minute.'

The men moved past them saying nothing, pretending they were not surprised to see Bess kiss him. Even Charley Klein turned his head as if realizing this was a private scene and he was trespassing upon it.

Dan put a hand under Bess's chin and tipped her head back. For a long moment he stared at her face that had been so familiar to him and now seemed different. For the first time in years he saw fear in Bess, and dread, and love. She was not the same woman he had known since her father's death, but maybe this was the real Bess Bailey. He thought it was.

'I love you,' he said in a voice so low that Charley Klein could not hear. 'And I'll be back. I promise.'

He kissed her again and strode out of the room, not looking back. The others were mounted by the time he stepped into the

184

saddle. He turned his horse toward Maroon canyon, the rest holding back and letting him take the lead. A moment later he saw a saddle horse in front of the teacherage.

Buffalo Jack Roman rode up beside him, asking, 'Dan, ain't that Jackson's sorrel?'

Dan waited until they reached the animal, then he was certain and he nodded agreement. 'It sure is. What do you make of it?'

'Dunno,' Roman said, 'but the chances are Jackson's in trouble. He's too good a rider to get throwed, though I guess it can happen to any man.'

'Fetch the horse along,' Dan said. 'We may find Jackson up here somewhere.'

They rode on, Roman leading Jackson's horse, Dan's gaze searching the trail ahead, then lifting to the rims above him. He saw nothing unusual until they were almost out of the canyon, then he spotted a man lying at the edge of the trail ahead of them.

'That'll be Jackson,' Dan said. 'Looks like he was throwed.'

'Knocked colder 'n a side of bacon, too,' Roman added.

Dan dismounted when they reached the man. It was Lee Jackson, his face gray except for the trace of blood on his lips. 'He's been shot,' Dan said. 'Bad.' He picked up a wrist and felt of the pulse. 'He's alive. Let's get him on his horse and take him to Margo's place. She'll nurse him.'

'I'll take him,' Roman said.

'Send Bess for her ma,' Dan said. 'She's the nearest thing to a doctor we've got.'

'You reckon the same bastard done this that got the others?' one of the men asked.

'Why would he?' Dan said.

No one gave him an answer. After he mounted and rode out of the canyon, Dan wondered if Jackson had actually decided to change sides, but someone would not let him. It could be the answer.

CHAPTER TWENTY-FIVE

As long as Dan was in the canyon with only the narrow slit of sky above him, he had not noticed how rapidly the storm clouds had moved in, but as soon as he led the column out of the walled confines of the canyon, he was aware of the flashes of lightning and the booming roll of thunder. He glanced up at the black sky, signaled for a halt, and dismounted.

'Them cattle are gonna be downright ringy,' one of the men said as they put on their slickers. 'Won't take much to make 'em run.'

Dan nodded, but he was thinking more of the Skull crew than he was of the herd. He wondered who was running the outfit, now that Lee Jackson wasn't with them, and how much fight would be in them. He swung back into the saddle and motioned the Hole men forward.

A short time later the rain hit, sweeping across the sage flat and bringing visibility close to zero. It was as if a silver screen had suddenly been drawn in front of them. They kept on riding, heads tipped forward, water running off their Stetsons and down their slickers.

The rain soon tapered off and Dan spotted the herd some distance to the east. One of the men said, 'There they are. Let's hit 'em.'

'No hurry,' Dan said. 'We've got a rider heading this way. Let's see if he wants to palaver.'

'We've got nothing to palaver about,' the rancher said harshly. 'Not after what they done to Carter and Willets. We've been on the wrong end of the stick too long. I say let's scatter that herd all over this end of Colorado.'

'We'll wait long enough to see if this man wants to talk,' Dan said. 'Once we open the ball, some of us are going to die. Maybe it won't be necessary.'

The man mumbled something. He wasn't convinced, but he stopped arguing. Dan held to his course so they would meet the incoming rider. The man must be heading for Smith's Hole, Dan thought, but he could not guess what sort of mission would bring one of Albright's men into the Hole.

It did occur to him that Buck Douglas had

heard about the murder of the two Texas men and was coming to investigate, but he discarded that possibility at once. It was unlikely that Douglas could have heard about the killings so soon.

The rider was within twenty feet of Dan before he recognized the man. He was Orly Hunt, and then Dan remembered Douglas saying that Hunt was riding for Skull and that it made no sense because he had retired several years ago.

Hunt pulled his horse up, calling, 'You're Dan Matson, ain't you?'

'That's right,' Dan answered, reining up and signaling for the men behind him to stop. 'It's been a long time since you've been in Smith's Hole, Hunt.'

'A long time,' Hunt agreed.

He was silent for a time, his gaze on Dan as if probing his reason for being here with the Hole men. Dan waited, thinking that if Orly Hunt represented Skull and Justin Albright, there was nothing formidable about him. He was a very wet and bedraggled old man.

'I was on my way to see you and your friends,' Hunt said. 'I figured you'd want to know that there ain't gonna be no trouble about Skull wintering in the Hole. Justin Albright is dead.'

At that moment nothing could have shocked Dan more than Hunt's last simple statement. Justin Albright with his power and wealth had seemed immortal. Dan had not even suspected that the man was here with his herd, but to know that he was here and was dead was more than he could comprehend in that first brief moment as he stared at Hunt.

'You're lying, mister,' one of the Hole men said. 'I don't believe it.'

'It's a trick,' a second man shouted. 'By God, we oughtta put a window in your skull for that.'

Hunt shrugged. 'I thought I was doing you a favor, but maybe you're just hankering for a fight. You can come on into camp and look at the body if you want to.'

'He ain't lying,' Dan said. 'How did it happen, Hunt?'

'You find Lee Jackson?' Hunt asked.

Dan nodded. 'He was lying beside the trail as we came up the canyon. How did that happen?'

'Albright came here from Denver expecting you men to have caved in,' Hunt said. 'He figured you'd be glad to take his offer. He blew up when he heard you hadn't and said we'd give you till tonight. If you hadn't taken his offer by that time, we'd shove the herd down Maroon canyon in the morning and kill any man who resisted. That was more 'n Jackson could take, so he cussed Albright and started to ride away, figgering to go see his girl, I reckon. Albright shot him in the back.'

'The hell,' Dan breathed, thinking this was

too incredible to be a lie.

'Jackson's been talking about quitting and he should have done it a long time ago,' Hunt went on. 'Anyhow, Albright was throwing down for a second shot when the first one didn't knock Jackson out of his saddle, but he never squeezed the trigger. The cook grabbed up his Winchester and put a bullet through Albright's head. Shooting Jackson was the biggest mistake Albright could have made. The men liked him, and nobody liked Justin Albright.'

Hunt took a long breath and shook his head. 'I figured that someday Albright would wind up with somebody's slug in him, but I sure never thought it would be one of his own men. Now I reckon we'll drive north to Rawlins and sell the herd. I've sent word to Judge Verling, who knows who Albright's heirs are, but that's his responsibility, not mine.'

Hunt started to turn his horse, then said, 'Keep a lookout for Kurt Sparks, Matson. He's been paid to dry gulch you. He's over there in the Hole now looking for you.'

'We'll find that son of a bitch,' one of the Hole men said as Hunt rode away. 'You don't need to worry, Dan.'

'Thanks,' Dan said, and turned back toward the head of Maroon canyon.

He was scared and he was irritated because it seemed to him that his neighbors sometimes acted as if they didn't have good sense. He'd better worry. He'd heard of Kurt Sparks, but he'd never heard anything good about the man. An experienced dry gulcher like that would be hard to find. He'd be a tough man to take once he was found. If he was cornered, the chances were good he'd wipe out half the male population of Smith's Hole before he was killed.

When Dan reached the head of the canyon, he discovered that Jack Roman was waiting on the trail that led to the top of Lone Rock. Roman motioned for Dan to join him. Dan reined off the road, telling the others he'd see them later.

'Jackson?' Dan asked as he pulled up beside Roman.

'He was alive when I left him,' Roman answered. 'What happened that brought you back so quick?'

Dan told him, adding, 'Now I've got to find Kurt Sparks before he finds me. I didn't know who it was that Albright had hired until Hunt told me.'

'Albright would hire the best,' Roman said, 'and I guess Sparks is the best, but you won't have to hunt for him. He's on the rim looking down at your place waiting for you to show.'

'So he's aiming to try it from the rim,' Dan said. 'I didn't think he would.'

'I guess he's a crack shot,' Roman said.

'How'd you know where he was?'

Roman jerked a thumb toward the top of Lone Rock. 'Ed Sanders is the lookout today.

When he saw me riding up the trail, he came down and met me here. He seen this jasper ride along the rim while ago, but he didn't pay no attention until Sparks kept stopping his horse back from the rim a piece and crawling to the edge like he was making damn sure nobody saw him from the Hole. When he got to where he could look down on your buildings, he stopped and stayed there. Ed couldn't see him during the storm, but when it cleared up, he said the bastard was still right there watching for you.'

'Then I'd better let him see me,' Dan said.

'I'll go with you,' Roman said. 'One man can't fight a grizzly. Hunting Kurt Sparks is the same thing.'

Dan shook his head. 'No, I need you here where you can watch him. I was thinking about it while you were talking. I figured I'd stay east of the ridge that follows the rim. He won't spot me if he's watching the ranch. All I want to do is to get close enough to get the drop on him and bring him in.'

'Or shoot the son of a bitch,' Roman said. 'He don't deserve no more trial than a rattler does who's just killed two men.'

'Depends on what he does,' Dan said. 'Anyhow, I want you to watch from Lone Rock. If he does see me and starts stalking me, fire one shot. If he stays there on the rim, don't do anything.'

'If that's the way you want to play it,'

Roman agreed reluctantly. 'I don't like the notion . . .'

Dan didn't wait for him to finish. He rode past Roman, angled east until he was behind the rocky ridge that paralleled the rim, then he rode north. He had often hunted here, so he was familiar with the country. When he reached a point directly east of his buildings, he reined up, dismounted, and tied. He had not heard a shot, so he assumed that Sparks was still waiting on the rim.

He slipped over the crest of the ridge, boots squishing in the mud. Once when he had a clear view through the cedars, he saw that Sparks was hunkered a few feet from the edge of the rim. He moved faster traveling down slope, knowing that any minute now Sparks would give up and turn away from the rim. When that happened, he would see Dan through the cedars and the fight would be in the open with Dan losing the advantage of surprise.

He reached the bottom of the ridge. The land leveled off here and was covered by a scattering of cedars. He was thankful that the rain had softened the twigs so they weren't snapping under his feet. He started to run. He had left his Winchester in the boot. At first he regretted not bringing the rifle, but the distance between him and Sparks diminished until he was close enough for his Colt to be effective.

'I'm Dan Matson,' he called. 'You looking for me, Sparks?'

Dan stopped, his cocked gun lined on the ambusher's back. Sparks froze, his Winchester in his right hand. Dan could guess what the killer was thinking, that after successfully following his murderous craft all these years, he had been caught from behind. There was no reason for it except overconfidence, the certainty that his victim would not know he was here and would eventually make his appearance at his ranch.

'Yeah, I want you, Matson,' Sparks said, still motionless. 'How'd you know I was here?'

'Our lookout spotted you from Lone Rock,' Dan said. 'Now drop your rifle and turn around. We'll hold you tonight in the Hole and take you to Craig tomorrow. I figure several states will fight over the privilege of hanging you.'

'You're wrong about that,' Sparks said. 'I'm not wanted in any state. I'm a careful man.'

'Until today,' Dan said.

'Even careful men make mistakes,' Sparks said. 'Now I'd make a dandy if I dropped my rifle and stood up and turned around. You'd shoot me in the belly, wouldn't you? You were a friend of Willets and Carter, weren't you?'

'I'm a friend of Charley Klein's, too,' Dan said. 'You beat him up for no reason. That's excuse enough to shoot you in the guts, but I won't. I'll take you in.'

'For your friends to hang,' Sparks said. 'I wouldn't live long enough to get to Craig. No, I'll stay this way. I've got an advantage on you. You wouldn't shoot a man in the back. I would.'

'All right, try me,' Dan said. 'Stay right where you are.'

He moved forward, watching the motionless man and expecting him to move. Still, Sparks almost caught him, so swiftly did he move, whirling and bringing his rifle up as he turned. He didn't quite get off his shot. Dan fired, the bullet catching Sparks in the side. The impact of the slug knocked him toward the rim.

Sparks dropped his Winchester and for a moment seemed to hang in space, his arms clawing at nothing more substantial than air, then he fell, his scream a shrill, terror-filled sound. Dan ran to the edge and looked down. What was left of Kurt Sparks lay sprawled on the rocks five hundred feet below the rim.

Dan holstered his gun and went back to his horse, realizing he was a free man with no threat hanging over him of a dry gulcher's bullet slamming into him from the next nest of boulders or screen of willows. He mounted and rode back to Roman who was waiting for him.

'I saw it,' Roman exulted. 'By God, he tried, even when he knowed you had him. He wasn't aiming to hang, though I reckon he didn't figure on going over the edge, neither.'

'No, I don't think he did,' Dan agreed.

They rode down Maroon creek together after calling Ed Sanders down from the top of Lone Rock. Bess saw them the instant they came out of the canyon. She ran toward them, crying, 'Dan, are you all right?'

He reined up the instant he reached her and swung down. 'Sure I'm all right,' he said as he took her into his arms. 'It's over, Bess. It's all over.'

She kissed him and then clung to him as if she was afraid she would still lose him. 'The last three or four hours have been the longest of my life,' she said. 'I thought I would never see you again.'

'Jackson?'

'Ma says he'll live.' Bess tipped her head back so she could see his face. 'Dan, I've got a mouthful of crow to eat. I've been too hard on Margo. She took Jackson in and says she'll nurse him back to life and then she'll marry him.'

'I told you she wasn't the way you thought she was,' Dan said.

Bess frowned, and for a moment he thought he had another argument on his hands, but instead, she laughed. 'You're not trapping me into play-acting again,' she said firmly. 'I honestly thought at one time that I wanted to be a man, but I've learned the hard way that I don't. I just want to be a woman, your woman.'

'Why,' he said, 'that's exactly what I want.

No more quarrels, no more fights, with you agreeing to everything I say.'

She shook her head. 'No. That would be one hell of a dull marriage, and you don't want that, do you?'

It was his turn to laugh. 'No, I don't. I just want Bess Bailey for my wife. No man could ask for more than that.'